PENNY'S STORY
A story of hope, optimism and love

Penny, fair and now far too slim, sat deep in thought, and the air of sadness that surrounded her was almost tangible.

It hadn't always been like this. Once the atmosphere had been warm and inviting, and then along came a silent assassin, and cruelly changed everything. A short while ago Penny had waved goodbye to the children – James at nineteen was in his second year at university and Lara, one year younger, was in her first year – and so, with plenty of time to think, she tried to come to terms with all that had happened.

Tall, dark and heavily built, Ben had been fifteen years older than Penny (he was just fifty when it all began). Kind, funny and enthusiastic, Ben's passion for cricket had once seen him thundering towards the batsman in the hope of getting his wicket; but when he was no longer 'fast', he had to bow to the inevitable and retire.

Luckily for Ben, all the family shared his love of the game, and it pleased him that James was keen to follow in his footsteps.

That morning it had been snowing, and Penny remembered thinking the consultant's voice was as soft and gentle as the snowflakes she watched falling outside his window. But their world fell apart when they heard him say that without chemotherapy Ben only had a few short months to live; and numb with disbelief, they never said a word.

Later the consultant took Ben into unknown territory.

Although he said he was cautiously optimistic, it was, however, going to be necessary to hammer him with the treatment, and that was the moment it all became too much.

One week later, in a bright and cheerful room, Ben waited for his chemotherapy to begin. Looking at the dozens of 'thank you' cards, he found the silence so unnerving. He felt he was sitting in an emotional no-man's-land.

The needle went into his gently held arm with laser-like precision. The bright-red liquid that flowed from the abnormally large syringe may have looked as innocent as a glass of red wine, but on the cancer cells it was intended to destroy it must have been as lethal as a time bomb.

At first they decided not to tell the children, but they knew there was going to be no shielding them from seeing their father so ill.

Already a competent athlete, James at nearly fourteen was tall and dark like his father; and Lara at twelve, with her mother's fair looks, was the apple of his eye.

So when they asked how they could help, Ben quietly said, "Just try and carry on as normal."

Like the unexpected fall of an avalanche, one dramatic crisis followed another.

As the mind-blowing drugs and savage chemotherapy took their toll, the treatment became more frightening than the illness.

This was a world where strengths and weaknesses, like open bleeding wounds, were publicly exposed to scrutiny, a dark and foreboding world where the human mind could sometimes descend into the depths of the most unimaginable despair.

Penny should have left it there, but she couldn't.

Finding the diary she kept during those months, she started to read each day's stark entry; and as she did so, she found herself reliving that day all over again. Urgently wanting to remember, and just as urgently not wanting to remember, she began to desperately flick over the pages.

Saturday 6th January
Ben said it was frightening to think of the devastation the cancer cells were causing – hopes to find the strength and determination to cope.

I said leave everything to me. He smiled and said he might find that one difficult!

Tuesday 9th January
Thought of gradually losing his hair quite alarming. Decided to have hair shaved. Young hairdresser arrived tonight and, after shaving Ben's hair, said a bald head was all the rage. Told him he looked like a nightclub bouncer, but it suited him!

Friday 12th January
Discussed whether to join a support group. Ben didn't think it wise: if he found people better than himself, he'd worry; and if worse, he'd wonder what was to come.

Sunday 14th January
Today, all his pent-up emotions surfaced, and with suffocating speed. Each word was a venomous indictment of this thing called cancer.

Calmer later, he said he couldn't bear the thought of leaving us. Bleak day.

Wednesday 17th January
Realize the uncertainty of this illness makes even the simplest thing difficult. Ben coping better.

Friday 19th January
Taken into hospital this morning. Very ill, in isolation.

Monday 22nd January
Doctor said after last week Ben must have the constitution of an ox. Chemotherapy had been very aggressive.

Tuesday 30th January
Came home very weak, mentally in a world of his own.

Wednesday 7th February
A big problem at the moment – every time a new set of symptoms appears, we wonder whatever is happening. Doctor says things will get easier.

Friday 16th February

Rushed into hospital. Sat with him and saw how he'd aged. Blood count low, slightly better tonight.

Sunday 18th February

While we were visiting, Ben had a violent shaking attack. When it was over I didn't want to leave – told to go home and rest. They said he would be fine.

Heard the next few months would feel like a journey into hell, but must think about the journey back. Easier said than done.

Thursday 22nd February

Ben home and much better – began to do a crossword. Not for long, but it didn't matter – it was a start.

Tuesday 27th February

This morning (without help) he's accomplished the mundane task of dressing himself – a big achievement. Thrilled.

Wednesday 6th March

With the reduction of some of his drugs, he's more like his old self, and the last few days have seen a semblance of normality. He says the train has finally run out of steam.

Monday 11th March

Blood count low – rushed into hospital. Better later.

Wednesday 13th March

Very poorly, in isolation. Just allowed to peep in. Was asleep.

Felt down, but the cheerful optimism of the doctors and nurses is astounding. Felt better later.

Thursday 21st March

Ben came home today. The Doctor has decided to try a course of injections (at home), and hopefully this will prevent the dramatic way his blood count drops.

Monday 1st April

Injections seem to be working – hasn't been taken into hospital.

Scan today. Ben appeared in blue gown, looked at the other patients in same gowns, and said whatever everyone's aspirations this is a great leveller.

Thursday 4th April

This morning the consultant's face was all smiles, leaning back in his chair. Heard the unbelievable words – the tumours had gone.

Saw the look of relief and sheer joy on Ben's face, and the solitary crystal-clear tear that fell slowly down his cheek. Shall never forget as long as I live.

Thursday 2nd May

Last chemotherapy. When the needle went into his arm, I hoped it was a symbolic gesture – this troubled chapter in his life is over.

Tuesday 28th May

Bank-holiday weekend. Ben rushed into hospital – suspect shingles. Very weak.

Disappointed his radiotherapy has been delayed.

Wednesday 5th June

Much better. Came home, but needs to have a catheter.

Thursday 6th June

Catheter blocked. Doctor and nurse came in the night, and eventually managed to unblock it.

Monday 10th June

Received his radiotherapy for the first time (daily for six weeks). Worried catheter might have delayed things again. Quite perky, but told he wouldn't be by Friday!

After putting the diary to one side, it wasn't long before she felt compelled to continue.

Sunday 16th June

Local marathon. Ben said he thought he'd never see this day. Remembered how he used to ask me, "What must you have to stay young?" And before I could answer he'd say, "Always have a dream." Well, today's been like a dream come true.

Monday 24th June

Drove himself to hospital – first time behind the wheel for six months. Felt proud of him, and now his depressing list of can't-do's is thankfully decreasing.

Wednesday 3rd July
Doctor not satisfied – sent for scan. All old anxieties returned.

Quickly confirmed: spleen and surrounding area OK. Thank God!

Saturday 13th July
Told to carefully shower area receiving treatment. So painful I heard him shout, "Bloody hell!"

Friday 19th July
Last radiotherapy. Coped well over the last weeks.

Monday 5th August
After four months, his irritating and unpredictable catheter was removed. It always baffled him, but it held a certain fascination, and sometimes his behaviour was rather comical.

Monday 26th August
For the last few weeks he's been indescribably tired, but slowly his need for sleep is becoming less urgent.

Sunday 8th September
Went to church for the first time since January. Ben said with hindsight the only way to live through the complexities of this illness was to live each day as it comes.

Tuesday 10th September
First of three monthly appointments at hospital. Doctor said everything fine, and Ben jumped off the bed in undisguised relief.

Friday 11th October
Spoke to the Doctor about his fear of the cancer returning. He said in the many years he's been in practice, he's never known this particular type to return.

Tuesday 10th December
Second three-monthly appointment. Doctor pleased. Scan January.

Friday evening 24th January
The hospital rang at 8pm! No sign of cancer. Ben said he is now the finished product, and, with a depth of emotion only the last year could have taught us, we are happy.

With the confirmation that he was in remission, nothing was taken for granted. Although he was sad the children had seen so much pain, he'd smile and say at least it often cut short their teenage tantrums.

Then, with the thought of how different things might have been, the next three years sped by.

Because it was still so horribly clear, she didn't need to read any more.

It had been nothing specific – just a general malaise – but for some time Ben hadn't been feeling well. Although he tried to ignore it, after a while he went to see his doctor, and immediately he was sent for an X-ray.

Over the years she had become used to hearing Ben say, "With this illness, Penny, it's always best to think the jury's still out," but that morning the consultant hadn't been his usual cheerful self, and, with two nurses in the room (this hadn't happened before), she had a terrible feeling something was seriously wrong.

As they listened to him go back to the beginning (and since they didn't need any reminding) his flat monotone voice seemed to hypnotize them. Then slowly the effect of his words led to a state of complete acceptance, and when his tone became almost a shaky whisper they were prepared for the worst.

The cancer had returned, and only palliative care was possible.

No one moved. No one spoke a word. There was a lack of emotion on Ben's inscrutable face. As she frantically looked around, imploring someone to say it wasn't true, her hold on Ben's hand became an iron grip of sheer determination, and she remembered thinking she didn't intend to let go without a fight.

Unaware her face was showing the pure unadulterated passion of the desperate (although she was screaming inside), she tried to remain calm, and then with every fibre of her being she reached out to them and pleaded, "Please – there must be something you can do?"

And, to be fair, they tried.

Two days later an unexpected course of chemotherapy was begun, but this time nothing could stop the breathtaking speed with which this cancer pursued its final objective. In one short heartbreaking week, Ben in all his gentleness was no longer with them. Just as he always feared, the sword of Damocles finally won.

Now, without Ben, she was just about managing the practical everyday mechanics of life, but only just.

While she operated on something like autopilot, her concentration was as familiar as a passing stranger. At the same time, she had to admit that people just could not win. There were those who, at a loss to know what to say, remained silent; others, with no such misgivings, skilfully avoided making any reference at all. But compared to the tea-and-sympathy brigade they were amateurs.

Now, it wasn't that Penny didn't appreciate people coming to see her – she did. In fact, she usually felt brighter and stronger after speaking to them. But she was finding that too much commiserating could be hard work, and sometimes after this type of visit she felt she had almost lost the will to live.

It hadn't helped that friends she had thought would be supportive, soon became 'telephone friends'. Conversations centred on "If it happened to me, I think I would just fall apart," and then, almost as an afterthought, ended with "You're being so brave."

Penny could only marvel at such mind-boggling insensitivity.

Then she discovered it was her and Ben's more distant friends who quietly moved to her side. Surprised to find she had so much in common with them, they soon became her dependable support system.

Without doubt the greatest help had come from the unobtrusive support of James and Lara. With no questions asked about their mother's erratic behaviour, they respected her wishes to do things her way. Since this frequently brought disastrous results, soon getting it wrong became the only teacher she knew. Showing a maturity beyond their years, they diplomatically said nothing.

Then, with a sensation as frightening as a sudden physical pain, Penny felt an intense longing to tell Ben all that had happened. In a desperate panic, she could only hope, as Ben had hoped, that if eternity really *was* just the passing of time, then perhaps in some unfathomable way he did know all that was happening.

Did he know, she wondered, how each day she systematically went through all her precious memories? And did he know her desperate need was fast becoming a powerful obsession? She could only fervently hope he did not.

That Penny found things extremely difficult went without saying, and not knowing what some people expected of her only added to her confusion. It was not surprising she was confused – she heard so many conflicting opinions on the state of bereavement. Some days she felt she was sinking in a whirlpool of well-intended advice.

However, when she was told to keep things 'simple' it sounded sensible, so she immediately tried to put it into practice.

One thing she was determined to try and avoid was the 'Why me?' syndrome. Although it hurt to remember why things were different, she had to try and find the courage to see that 'different' was where she had to begin.

One morning Penny received an unexpected phone call from Hillary, a counsellor at the local hospice.

Hillary said the reason for her call was to see if Penny would like to come to their bereavement-group meetings, which were held on the last Thursday evening of the month. This was an invitation that was extended to everyone who had lost a loved one at the hospice. Hillary asked Penny if she would like to think about it, and, if she thought it might help, she would look forward to seeing her.

The meetings took place in an annexe at the back of the hospice, and the car park was directly in front of the entrance.

Penny quickly decided she would at least give it a try, and she hoped that it might help with her new-found irrational fears.

Sitting in her car, Penny looked at the door, where inside she had been told the meetings took place, and, contrary to what she had expected, she was not in the least nervous. In fact she was just hoping that here she would find the practical help that she so badly needed.

Almost immediately, as Penny walked into the room, a pretty young lady with long dark hair quickly came to her and introduced herself as Hillary, who had spoken to her on the phone, and Penny thought she didn't look anything like she had thought a counsellor would look like. (But then of course she had absolutely no idea how a counsellor would look.)

With a colourful beaded headband and bright and sparkly top, just looking at Hillary raised your spirits.

A few minutes later a young man joined them, saying he was Phil, the other counsellor. With a slightly droopy moustache and a small beard, his rather solemn manner was strangely comforting. After chatting for a while, Phil excused himself and said he would mingle.

Afterwards Hillary said one of Phil's biggest strengths was his ability to carefully listen, and this was one of the many things that made him so popular and well liked.

Looking around the large room, Penny could see a long table in the middle, where five or six rather noisy people were sitting close together, obviously enjoying themselves. On either side of this long table there were three small round tables, and by contrast the people sitting at these tables were all quietly engrossed in apparently earnest conversation. On one side of the room was an open hatch, and Penny could see the cups and saucers and plates of biscuits all waiting patiently for the evening 'break'.

When Hillary had introduced Penny to practically everyone, Penny could only manage to put a few names to faces. One was Margaret – she sat at the top of the long table, looking very much in charge. Still very attractive, she had short blonde hair, and looked somewhere in her middle sixties. By her side sat Aubrey, with white curly hair and a deep commanding voice. He was still a good-looking man. Yet it didn't take much perception to see that lurking not very far away was someone with a considerably large ego. Penny had to admit that when Hillary had introduced her Aubrey had been (if a little distracted) very friendly, but then Margaret had seemed to be monopolizing him. Some of the other names Penny could remember were Aggie, June and Maurice.

Then Hillary said, "Come with me. I think you'll like sitting with Patsy and Ethel."

They were both quite tall and slim, but that's where the similarity came to an abrupt halt. Patsy's hair was still a chestnut brown and her short, tight curls a perm. On the other hand Ethel's hair was iron grey, and cropped so close to her head it looked almost masculine.

Ethel just said, "It's less trouble."

In other circumstances they could well have been a comical double act, so Penny was not surprised to find they were also close friends. Twice a year they went on holiday together – their social life consisted of doing everything together.

At one of the first meetings they had attended at the hospice, they found both their husbands had passed away on the same day, and this seemed to have cemented their friendship. Their natures complemented each other. Patsy led, and Ethel was more than happy to follow. Penny knew all this within no time at all, and she could see why Hillary had taken her to their table. From the outset Penny had liked them. It would have been almost impossible *not* to like them. They were easy company, and Penny felt she had always known them.

After Hillary had given a short talk (Patsy said Hillary and Phil took it in turns to speak at the meetings), Hillary asked if there were any questions. There were none, so she added that if anyone would like to speak to her or Phil in private, they could use the room at the end of the corridor.

Hillary's little talk had been about keeping things simple, and it was only with the passing of time that things slowly began to feel more normal. She also said things will be different, but was different so dreadful?

Penny had been told about time before, but she never tired of hearing it. It could be that it always seemed to help more when it came from strangers.

One other thing Penny had found interesting was when Hillary said she was often asked how long the despair and uncertainty lasted, and Hillary said her answer was always the same: bereavement affects people in many different ways, but, generally, nature and the sort of relationship you had with your loved one is usually the key to how you cope.

Patsy and Ethel said that most people who came to the meetings were either retired or about to retire. Then in chorus they both said, "But you're young, Penny, and hopefully you'll make another life for yourself. Most of us come for the company, and help if we need it. You come, Penny, as long as you feel you're getting something good out of it."

And Penny knew that was just what she would do.

But now Penny's curiosity was getting the better of her, and since she had found Aubrey intriguing she asked Patsy about him. Patsy said that Margaret had once said he had been a 'big fish in oil', and Penny did her best to keep a straight face. Once Aubrey had showed Margaret a wedding photograph of his late wife and himself, and she said his wife had been really attractive, but a frail little thing. They had no children, so Margaret thought Aubrey was quite lonely.

Then Patsy took a deep breath and sniffed as she said, "Some of that lot on the long table have been coming here for years. I don't know why – they're probably hoping to meet somebody." Then, sniffing again and with a great deal of knowing scepticism, Patsy sarcastically said, "Well, up to now none of them have had much luck!"

And Penny thought, 'Oh dear – what does Patsy know?'

On the way home Penny thought how friendly they had all been, and listening to their stories had, in a funny sort of way, made her feel better about herself.

Preparing for another first, Penny got into her car and began the familiar journey to work.

Along a busy main road, and within a mile or so of each other, her route took her through all the six small industrial towns of the city. With the countryside only a ten-minute drive away, to a stranger unaware of this geographical phenomenon everything must have looked rather daunting and depressing.

With a few years' break when the children were small, Penny had worked at Farrington's for twenty years. As the children grew more independent, she gradually increased her hours.

Before the arrival of the supermarkets and chain stores, the garage had stood in almost splendid isolation. With large gold letters displaying the Farrington name, the prestigious showroom completely dominated the front of the long, low building.

The offices at the back of the garage, if not exactly state of the art, were modern and comfortable, and the parts department was run with army-like precision by Brian, a small wiry bachelor and a stickler for detail.

Sam, the service manager, was a burly red-faced man. The few strands of hair he had left he placed in an alarming criss-cross over the top of his bald head, and, whatever the weather, that's how they stayed.

Sam had been at Farrington's since a boy, and there was little he didn't know about the business; and what he didn't, he soon made it his business to find out. Because of this, his decisions were usually considered sacrosanct and rarely queried. That was until a few years ago, when a young naive mechanic had the audacity to do just that, and Sam was so affronted it unhinged him for days.

Farrington's paint shop was the domain of Tony, tall, gangly and for most of the time humble in manner. He appeared to be ill-equipped to deal with anything that moved faster than a snail, but that would be to underestimate Tony. He knew his job and did it well, and his affable approach won him many friends. Though his splattered paint-shop walls looked like the work of a contemporary artist, Tony's department had few problems.

Since Charles had been groomed from an early age, it was not surprising that when Edgar Farrington (a difficult and enigmatic man) retired the transition from father to son took place with such ease it hardly caused a ripple.

Over the years, as Charles's large frame became ever more cumbersome, so his intriguing gait became more noticeable. While his right foot always found the ground with unerring accuracy, the rest of his body appeared reluctant to follow. He had thick unruly hair – most people couldn't remember it as anything other than as white and fluffy as cotton wool.

To those who knew him well, he was a kind and considerate

15

man; his brusque and intimidating manner was all part of a cultivated image that had served him well. To those who didn't, he was a typical businessman – one who for many years had been the undisputed force behind the success of Farrington's.

Charles had always treated his staff like an extended family, and since his wife, Daphne (who still retained her waif-like prettiness), had been a frequent visitor, she was as popular as Charles. Now he had finally retired. His only child, Max (a lecturer in economics in London), had always been reluctant to succeed him, and the reason for his change of mind was anybody's guess. There was more than a little trepidation at the prospect of his imminent arrival.

Max Farrington was a tall, slim and aloof man. Although most said he was scrupulously polite, he did have a distinct air of indifference. The last time he had been into Farrington's his hair was noticeably grey.

Somewhere in his late forties, he had never married, but according to rumour and office gossip he had once been engaged. As to what went wrong, no one ever found out.

After that, depending on whose version you listened to, he either took no further interest in women, or, as others knowingly suggested, he took far too much interest. Whatever the truth, he was now the new head of the company.

With desk-lined walls and three large desks in the middle of the floor, the accounts department was the largest office at Farrington's. The accountant, Nigel, had his office sectioned off by a glass sliding partition, and there was not much he missed. The fact he had little or no privacy was a constant bone of contention, and when he was having a particularly bad day he said it was like working in a bloody goldfish bowl. With a deep guttural voice and aquiline features, he was good-looking and he knew it.

Greg, his assistant, was Nigel's complete antithesis. His long bony face was not in the least bit attractive, but he was kind and patient.

Dot and Molly cleared the suppliers' invoices for payment. There were never two more different characters. Dot, small and plump, had a preference for long flowing skirts and frilly blouses, and Molly, tall and stylish, had a rather off-putting manner. But they knew how to compromise, and they worked well together.

Simon and Nick were the computer experts. While Simon was the office charmer, you could always rely on Nick for the amusing one-liner.

Colin, a quiet and methodical man, combined the payroll with that of office manager, and Beth, dark and pretty, was the office junior.

Although Penny had dreaded walking into the office, when she did, everybody was so natural the difficulties she anticipated just never happened.

When she went to see Nigel (he liked to be the first to impart any news, and if he wasn't it had been known for him to sulk all day) he brought her up to date on the events of the last few weeks.

Unusually, he said he'd leave it to the others to tell her about Charles's departure (and that meant it went without a hitch).

The next day, Max Farrington gathered all the staff in the canteen, and, much to everyone's surprise, he said it would be some time before he was there on a permanent basis, but in the meantime he could see no reason for any problems.

Charles Farrington had enjoyed the personal touch, and he'd known the names of all his staff, but Nigel didn't think the same would apply to Max. He suspected if the job was done satisfactorily, then that would be that.

At the end of the day, Penny was too busy to think about anything other than her work, and she felt pleased to be back. But it was quite another story when, driving home, she thought how different things were going to be. Now instead of James and Lara both wanting to be the first to say, "Mum – guess what?" and then half an hour later Ben arriving, tonight there would be no one to want anything, and all over again the 'if onlys' began. Realizing all the 'if onlys' in the world couldn't alter things, she simply dreaded walking into the house.

When she did, it was even worse than she imagined. She was met by an atmosphere so cold and indifferent, she morbidly thought, 'If this house lived and breathed, I'd say it had lost its very soul.'

Quickly pulling herself together, she said out loud, "Please, God, let it get better."

Whether it did get better or she just got better at it she didn't know, but gradually, as the weeks drifted by, she quietly accepted this was how it had to be.

While she was the first to acknowledge that the routine and discipline of work was just the therapy she needed, on some days she would have given anything to be at home; and then on other days she couldn't wait to be on her way. This made her accept the unpalatable truth that (however out of character) she had now joined the annoying ditherers' club.

Although she had been assured there were many advantages in living alone, Penny didn't expect to find any. She was more inclined to think the vast majority of people (unless an alternative came along) eventually came to terms with the situation and just got on with it.

But she was finding being accountable to herself was bringing its own problems. For instance, she seemed to have acquired all the necessary qualifications to gain a Masters degree in changing her mind; and sometimes when she said she would be doing one thing, she knew, even while she was saying it, she probably wouldn't be doing it at all. So when she was invited to spend an evening with friends, it sent her into a complete spin. After days of uncertainty she looked to Ben for the answer; and knowing he would have said, "Go," that was what she did. But she did wonder if she would always feel this desperate need to please him in this way.

When the day arrived, she finally decided to wear the plain blue dress he had always liked, with a neckline just low enough to be discreet. It had a classic straight skirt, to which she added a broad belt and long chain. She also put on her high-heeled black court shoes. This was the first time she had dressed for an evening without Ben, and looking in the mirror she was pleased with the effect.

Then suddenly, without any warning, she felt she was being suffocated. She pulled at the belt and literally ripped off the dress. Shaken to the core by her violent reaction, she couldn't believe she had even contemplated going out in a dress that held so many memories.

Taking a straight white skirt and plain black top from the wardrobe, she put them on, and without a backward glance she went downstairs, picked up her handbag and went outside to the car.

Almost overpowering her with their kindness, everyone seemed really pleased to see her, so why after asking "How are you?" and "Are you coping?" and "Are things getting any easier?" did nobody wait for her to answer? Instead she was quickly asked, "Have you heard about Don Bevington?"

He had been in Penny's form at school; and when she said she hadn't, she found herself listening to all the complicated details of his recent divorce.

She did try to enjoy the evening, but somehow she couldn't begin to find the wavelength of the light-hearted banter, and she came to the conclusion only a masochist would have put herself through such torture. If it was not an unmitigated disaster, then her first social foray had hardly been encouraging.

It was not that Penny had any desire to subject people to a blow-by-blow account of how she was feeling, but she couldn't fail to notice that when some people asked they never waited for her to answer.

A few days later, she decided that maybe friends seeing her on her own felt as uncomfortable as she did.

She knew her values were not the same, because what had once seemed to be important now appeared almost trivial. Since her well-practised and unpredictable emotions were threatening to run away with her, she decided to confide in her elderly Auntie Kitty.

Understanding and kind, Auntie Kitty was very fond of Penny, and she tried to answer all her questions honestly. She told Penny the only safe way was to live through all her sadness, and then in time things would become easier.

She said, "Of course Ben's death will have changed you, but you have the children, Penny, and life has to go on."

After their long chat, Penny did feel it had helped, and she knew Auntie Kitty's advice had really been just plain common sense.

One morning the computers were down, and Simon and Nick's expletives echoed around the office.

Colin sympathized and Greg looked up and laconically remarked, "Problems?"

While Penny preferred to let them get on with it, Dot and Molly were definitely not at their best. Dot tutted (their colourful language often upset her) and Molly, with a face like thunder, showed her disapproval by sitting even more erect at her desk. Clearly finding it difficult not to say more than a disdainful "Really!" she proceeded to give Beth (who was struggling with the hinges on a broken file) her undivided attention.

Suddenly Simon gave a loud groan: "Bloody hell – it's Arthur Dagshaw."

Sure enough, a few minutes later Arthur walked into the office. Now, 'walked' is a very loose interpretation, because, depending on which angle you happened to witness the unfortunate incident from, he either stumbled, shuffled or literally fell.

Over the years everyone had become inured to his rather dramatic entries, and as they all said "Good morning, Mr Dagshaw" no one even bothered to look up from their desks.

This was followed by Arthur's "Mornin'."

From past experience it was necessary to appear as frantically busy as possible; otherwise he was inclined to outstay his welcome, or, as Nigel so delicately put it, "He bloody well takes root."

A farmer, he always paid his considerably large account in the most musty foul-smelling banknotes, and each month they were put unceremoniously on to Penny's desk. As she went to count them, he would say, "No need to check it, lass." But it was Penny's unenviable task to make sure it was all correct.

Arthur was one of Farrington's oldest customers, and in all those years no one had ever seen him in anything other than his green cord baggy trousers. Consequently, they had become as much of an institution as Arthur himself. After one visit Nick mused that they were either his 'Farrington trousers' or they were a masterpiece of craftsmanship.

This morning it was Penny who had his undivided attention, and there was no doubting his concern.

"I've missed yer, lass. How are things?"

Penny said it helped to keep busy, and he nodded his head in approval.

Then almost to himself he said, "See – you're young."

"Not that young, Mr Dagshaw," Penny politely replied.

With that, in a voice so solemn you would have thought he was about to divulge the very secret of life, Arthur said, "I'll tell yer what, lass: in a yard full o' tractors, yow'd be the Rolls-Royce."

Wondering where on earth that came from, Penny looked surprised, and then, seeming pleased with himself, he veered towards the door, and left.

Stopping on his way to inform Dot, it was no wonder he had high blood pressure. Sam made a beeline for Simon and Nick.

He demanded to know if the computers would be up and running, and then added without pausing for breath, "Do you realize what is going on downstairs?" He almost choked.

"Very little" was the correct answer, because until the computers were back on track there was very little anyone could do.

Realizing this was one of the reasons for Sam's annoyance, they tried to console him, but Sam ignored them.

Warming to his theme, he addressed the office in what Greg described as Sam's 'special occasions' voice: "After Christmas," he announced, "Max Farrington will be here permanently."

"How do you know that?" was everyone's quick response.

Satisfied he now had a captive audience, he continued: "Never mind, but I have it on good authority."

That meant Charles Farrington had told him.

By now it was obvious Sam was feeling really peeved, and he glared at Simon and Nick.

"Things will be different in here when Max Farrington arrives."

"How?" everyone wanted to know.

"He'll sort you lot out, that's how."

Then, having grown tired of the whole matter, he grumbled all the way to the door.

Nowadays, when Penny went to the supermarket she usually looked at the food on the shelves with little more than a lethargic interest. Then, at the checkout, conscious she was shopping for one, she would spread her purchases thinly along the conveyor belt.

Tonight, with James and Lara home for the weekend, she went around the aisles with an enthusiasm she thought had long gone, and at the till she couldn't believe how much she had bought. Filling one plastic bag after another, she never remembered doing her shopping with so much pleasure, and she wondered why she had always made it such a chore. Given the chance she decided things would be different.

But of course they wouldn't. If time was a great healer, it also had the vision to glamorize the mundane.

On the Saturday afternoon she went into town with Lara, and James did all the heavy work in the garden. Then in the evening, while they met their friends, Penny busied herself preparing for Sunday's lunch.

With family and friends around on the Sunday evening, Penny spent most of the time thinking 'If only!'

Before James and Lara left, they had a long talk with Penny. More than once they said whenever they had a problem, they just thought how Dad would have dealt with it, and it always helped.

Alone, and with no one to break the awful silence, she was unable to stop herself from going over everything again.

When Ben died, she had wanted to shield the children from all the sadness, but she had been so consumed by her own grief, and now she felt she hadn't given them the undivided attention they had the right to expect.

Looking back, James and Lara appeared to have been far more resilient than she had. Although family and friends had given them their unquestioning support, she still felt she hadn't been strong enough.

At the time they had talked for hours, and Penny thought that was the best thing to do, but now she wondered if it had been enough.

By the middle of November, the dark evenings, the dangers of fireworks and the sadness of Remembrance Day were no longer topics of conversation, but she needn't have worried – with the help of those who knew all about 'these things', the perils of Christmas were next on the list.

In the meantime (offering additional help and support) there was the annual bereavement service at church, and this year the speaker had the unusual name of Chastie Hope. After reading the following, Penny decided to go along.

> I found bereavement deeply personal and emotionally lonely, and I came to realize there could be no arrival time on the diverse and complex journey I felt compelled to make.
>
> Then I made the comforting discovery I was not alone, and my experiences and confused emotions were all part of a universal truth, shared by everyone who had lost someone they loved.

Penny walked into the church hall, and was surprised to see so many familiar faces. For some reason she thought this was the kind of evening you came to once, and then wouldn't want to repeat.

The vicar, in his gushing introduction, made her feel quite uneasy. Surely it was a bit misleading to give the impression that Chastie Hope was about to wave a magic wand, and everyone's fears and anxieties would disappear. But at times the vicar did have this tendency to get carried away.

Penny remembered the Sundays his sermons seemed to go on forever, and then he began to fall into the trap of repeating himself.

When this happened, Ben would whisper, "For heaven's sake, he's a good turn, but he's on too long!"

Tall and buxom, Chastie Hope wore a dark tailored suit and a crisp white blouse. From the moment she walked on to the stage, Penny had the distinct feeling this was a lady you certainly didn't mess around with. Standing imperiously before her audience, she spoke with ease and familiarity on a subject she was obviously well versed in.

She began by saying there were no short cuts in bereavement. Then, speaking in detail about the effects of time, she said she was frequently asked, "Well, how much time does it take?" And she said this depends entirely on the person and the type of relationship they had with their loved one. She then went on to say that feeling unsettled was natural, and keeping busy was crucial, and she fluently described the despair, loneliness and sadness of bereavement. (By now Penny had lost track of what was being said, or maybe she had just stopped listening.) With the skill of a surgeon, Chastie Hope was thoroughly dissecting each and every manifestation of grief. Now, after speaking for over an hour with all the authority of the Almighty, she finally concluded with "Any questions?"

And there were none.

With her powers of persuasion, Penny thought she had all the charisma of an enthusiastic evangelist, and she couldn't help feeling that a conversation with Chastie Hope would be nothing short of a mountaintop experience. But since Penny had heard these things many times in the last few months, she still found Hillary's upbeat and realistic message far more uplifting and encouraging. It was times like this that made Penny pleased that she still went to the bereavement meetings. And now, after three months, along with the help of Hillary, Patsy and Ethel (in fact everyone), she was beginning to understand that never far from the surface, and making difficult moments easier, she had an irrevocable self-deprecating dark humour. Penny had begun to notice that some people were slowly drifting away, and she wondered if these short intense friendships (unless they discovered a mutual interest) were never intended to be anything more than 'ships that pass in the night'. It took Patsy in her down-to-earth way to point out that the purpose of the group was to give help and support, and the confidence to slowly move on.

No longer one of life's imponderables, Max Farrington would be officially joining the company at the beginning of January.

Greg's matter-of-fact response was a rather bored "Well, that's one more topic of conversation that bites the dust."

On the occasions he did come into the garage, Max's time was usually spent with Nigel, and then after a while he would ask to see Frank, the sales manager, and lastly Sam appeared. He had very little contact with anyone else.

As Dot dryly put it, "Why should he? Nigel's the accountant, Frank has the car sales figures and Sam – well, let's face it, Sam knows everything."

Looking more like an annexe than part of the original structure, the boardroom and Max Farrington's office were situated at the far corner of the building, and, adding insult to injury, the only access was by using the accounts department as a general thoroughfare.

Colin, with the pained air of someone who had seen it all before, thought old Edgar Farrington must have been mad to have agreed to this (in his opinion) architectural disaster. But it had suited Charles Farrington, because most days, on his way either in or out, he would invariably stop to chat with someone.

Dot didn't think this was going to please Max Farrington at all, but before she could say any more, and knowing exactly how to wind her up, Simon winked at Nick and said, "Tough, Dot!"

Now, at times like this Dot would display her hurt look, and she rather petulantly said, "I wouldn't mind, Simon, if you tried to be a little more respectful."

Simon's answer, although intended to humour, only made matters worse: "It's not really like that any more."

Thereupon Molly, quick as a flash, scathingly said, "So we've noticed."

With only Penny in the office at lunchtime, Nigel came and ate his sandwiches with her. After asking how she was finding things, she briefly told him about Chastie Hope. (A couple of years ago, his wife had left him, and recently his divorce had gone through.) He said in an article he had read, bereavement and divorce had come at the top of the list of stressful events, and for the first time Penny felt he was beginning to come to terms with what had happened.

For the rest of the lunchtime they spoke about their experiences. It seemed once he'd begun to open up, he was finding it difficult to stop.

Then casually he said, "We're in similar boats, you and me – why don't we go out for a meal sometime?"

She must have looked so shocked.

Nigel gave her a reassuring smile and said, "Don't worry – maybe when you're ready?"

When Lara rang, Penny told her about Nigel, adding that he was nothing like her father.

"But, Mum," Lara said, "you're not going to meet another Dad." Then, warming to the situation she found herself in, she said, "Look – he's different. Now, that's not necessarily a bad thing, and – for goodness' sake, Mum – he's only asked you if you would like to go out for a meal!"

Things were changing too quickly for Penny.

Frank, the sales manager, was tall and suave with an iron-grey moustache. He had a temperament very much the same as Sam's. But it was his moustache that revealed the most about Frank. On a good day it never moved, but under pressure it seemed to have a will of its own. If his moustache was seen to twitch, then most people were clever enough to keep out of his way. For years he had stubbornly done things his way, and no amount of persuasion from any quarter had ever had the slightest effect. His sales sheets were a nightmare to decipher, and Nigel said he only had to take one look and he could feel one of his debilitating headaches coming on.

Tristan, with his slightly balding hair and well-rehearsed theatrical gestures, considered himself to be one of Farrington's most valuable assets, and he liked to give the impression he was destined for greater things. According to Greg he deluded himself on both counts, but he could sell cars. With a vocabulary that just about stopped short of interesting, he was the expert on talking about nothing at all – that was until he came to (his words) his 'four-bed detached and two garages'. Then he really could wax lyrical.

Eclipsed by Tristan and in awe of Frank, Mark was the junior salesman. To everyone's amusement, Dot once likened the colour of his hair to that of sunlight on pure gold (but Dot did enjoy reading a good love story).

Today under Frank's eagle eye the showroom had been transformed for Christmas, and he'd done it with the expertise of a veteran. Each year everyone would agree that the decorations couldn't be done better, only to find the following year Frank did just that. In the artificial snow, the tiny white lights flickered like dancing stars, and hanging from the strategically placed Christmas trees the silver-coloured lanterns looked for all the world like sparkling priceless gems.

But somehow Penny didn't quite see it like that, and for one dreadful moment those tiny white lights had reminded her of a thousand smiling tears.

On the way home, she wondered why she always looked for sadness in everything, and she began to think the warnings she had received on the perils of Christmas were probably true. Having acquired enough well-intended advice to fill a book, she didn't understand why she always forgot to put any of it into practice.

While it had been a relief to hear, it was natural to suddenly feel tearful when she was told an irreverent sense of humour could sometimes help. She had already found that out for herself.

When things became really difficult, her 'uncharitable thoughts' (from the quite simply ridiculous to the downright vindictive) became the defence mechanism for all her fragile emotions.

For those with no reason to be part of the commercialized frenzy, it was easy to see why Nigel said Christmas was the worst time for those who are bereaved.

"Every bloody shop you go into", he said, "reminds you you're on your own."

But Penny intended to be as philosophical as she could. In truth, the sooner it was over the better, but in the meantime she would grit her teeth and get on with it. With the children home this weekend (they could do the tree), she was aware she had a lot to be thankful for, and this spurred her into action.

The Christmas cards' bright and cheerful greetings seemed to mock in open defiance the way she felt, so she had decided to have nothing to do with them; but now, after hesitating for only a second and thinking about Ben, she carefully arranged them on the walls.

Ben had always enjoyed attending to the Christmas cards, but his relationship with the Christmas-tree lights had always been rather turbulent. When they would refuse to give even a glimmer of hope, he lost his temper.

Surprised at herself for thinking about Ben like this, she felt disloyal and even guilty, and then she thought of the time a friend had said, "Don't try and make Ben seem perfect, Penny. None of us are."

Looking at the cards, she gave a wry smile. Although her interest had only been fleeting, it had been a start. Then, thinking about Ben again, her tummy gave a quick somersault.

When he had died, Penny could only think, 'Why now? We all need you.' But slowly – ever so slowly – she was beginning to understand that it would never have been the 'right' time. They would always have wanted longer.

Penny didn't quite know whether it was design or accident, but there was definitely something strange going on, and she wondered why nearly everybody she spoke to seemed to have this urgent need to share their domestic bliss. With admirable skill and ingenuity, the conversations were soon manoeuvred into a position of attack.

"I don't know what I'd do if I lost my husband, wife, companion or partner, they'd remark," and then in hushed tones they'd proceed to give their loved ones a glowing verbal reference.

Sometimes, Penny wished she had the courage to say, "Fine – just don't tell me." But instead, with a vengeance that took her breath away, she put her 'uncharitable thoughts' into practice.

The Christmas dinner and dance was usually a talking point for weeks beforehand, and, depending on the outcome, it could still be a talking point well into the middle of January. Against her better judgement, Penny had been persuaded to go.

While Charles and Daphne Farrington would be there, it was anyone's guess about Max, but Molly didn't think he was the type for Christmas do's.

Pulling her chair even further away from her desk, she pronounced, "From what I've seen, it would frighten the life out of him."

Nigel and Simon didn't agree. In fact they both thought he could be a bit of a ladies' man.

Thereupon Molly quickly retorted, "Well, if anybody should know, you two should!"

On the days Dot felt the need to exercise her authority, she drew back her long dark hair and piled it on the top of her head into the most enormous bun. Since the height and sight of it was not for the faint-hearted, it was no wonder it made Nigel think about his vertigo. At the end of the month, she was always on form.

This morning, in an effort to see all the invoices were cleared for payment, she was due to make her monthly visit to each department, and, although she protested this was part of her job she disliked, everyone secretly thought she actually enjoyed it. (Otherwise, in her own inimitable way she would have passed it on to Molly.)

Since most departments were guilty of not clearing their paperwork on time, it was up to Dot to see things were dealt with promptly. That she was so successful was probably due to the fact she took most things in her stride, and when she didn't she did it with such well-practised ease that she rarely ruffled anyone's feathers.

When Brian appeared, he made straight for Dot's desk. Nick looked at him knowingly and shook his head.

"Your girlfriend doesn't seem very pleased today."

Immediately, Brian started to blink furiously and Dot shot Nick a withering look.

Then Brian, with the air of someone about to get his own back, suddenly turned to Nick and said, "Didn't I see you with Angela last night?"

Now, unfortunately for Nick, Angela was a near neighbour of Brian's.

"Angela who?" everyone wanted to know.

Now it was Nick's turn to look embarrassed.

"Just someone I've taken out a few times, that's all."

At thirty-two, that was as far as Nick ever got.

Then, going straight for the jugular, Brian asked, "Did you know she has three kids?"

"Two," corrected Nick.

"I think," Brian said ominously, "you'll find it's three."

By now, with the attention diverted to Nick, Dot was enjoying herself.

"Oh, Nick, do be careful."

"Don't be soft, Dot – it's nothing serious," but he did look uncomfortable.

Wondering what was going on, Nigel came out of his office.

"Come on, folks – we're not a lonely hearts club. Let's get some work done."

At lunchtime, Penny went into town with Dot. Apart from her outrageous bun, she did have one other idiosyncrasy, and that was her liking for impossibly high-heeled shoes. This made walking, in the strictest sense, a near impossibility, so that an hour around the shops with Dot was very much like an endurance test. But in one respect today was different, because for the first time she acknowledged that Brian would like to take her out. (In her thirties, Dot lived at home with her widowed mother.)

Implying after what had happened to Penny she should try to make a life for herself, she said, "Well, I'm not going to have Mother forever, am I?"

Penny agreed, and Dot left it at that.

Since it was obvious she would like to go out with Brian, Penny couldn't help thinking what a frustrating pair they were.

"For heaven's sake," she wanted to shout, "get on with it and try and make each other happy."

Thinking about it later, she didn't understand why it had made her feel so irritated. After all, the 'Will she? Won't she?' cliffhanger of Dot and Brian had long been a source of mild amusement at Farrington's.

All this made Penny realize how much she was changing. She was finding that without Ben all her decisions had to be her own, and, after sharing everything for so long, it wasn't an easy lesson to learn.

With so many poignant memories, it was hardly surprising Penny found going to church so upsetting. During Ben's illness, the church and their friends in the congregation had all been a great support. They had witnessed the joys and the sadness, the optimistic times and the terrible final weeks. Small wonder when afterwards, as she sat through a church service, she had for one wishful heart-stopping moment thought how different things might have been.

Now, six months later, she decided to try again.

Typical of its age and architecture, the small Victorian church looked as indestructible as the faith it bore witness to, but over the years a lot of work had been needed to maintain it and comply with safety regulations.

Standing at the top of a steep incline, it had once been surrounded by green fields and open countryside, but not any more. Now it had the dubious company of several shops, a social club and a modern housing estate.

Slipping unnoticed into church, she was pleased no one had seen her arrive, and, still not entirely at ease, she went to sit in the back row.

Before long (just as she knew it would) Ben's presence became almost palpable. Most people had seen Penny arrive, but, understanding the next hour was not going to be easy, they wisely (until after the service) remained in the background. With her emotions as taut as the strings of a finely tuned violin, she looked at the sheer simplicity of the altar, and for some reason the pure white altar cloth reminded her of a choirboy wearing his vestments for the very first time.

Quickly coming down to earth, she couldn't understand why everything was having such a profound effect – after all, nothing had changed. But then she became painfully aware that she had.

After the service, she was overwhelmed by her friends' invitations to go out one evening, but although she thanked them she had little inclination to get involved. Maybe it was a lack of confidence, but the thought of socializing was like a real-life nightmare.

This was so unlike how she used to be, but without Ben she had no heart for anything.

Sometimes she felt she was having to relearn everything, but at the same time she wasn't really making a very good job of it.

Perhaps if she could show just a little more interest and enthusiasm (at the moment she never noticed who walked into or out of her life), it might make her feel better. This time, Penny told herself, she really had to try.

Then much sooner than she expected, and way before she was ready, she was put to her first test.

Penny and Julie had been friends since their teens, and over the years the trials and tribulations of Julie's varied and colourful love life had been graphically described in phone conversations that required a certain amount of stamina.

A complete extrovert, Julie was extremely attractive. She had thick, dark shoulder-length hair, and she applied her make-up with a generosity that would have put a champion philanthropist to shame. Maybe 'subtle' was not in her nature. A legal secretary with a local firm of solicitors, although (as yet) she hadn't married, she had never been short of boyfriends. Some had been more than suitable, some disastrous, and others in an ideal world would have been strictly out of bounds.

Ben used to say she was her own worst enemy, and, although Penny hadn't liked him saying so, she had to reluctantly agree it was true.

One night she rang and asked Penny if she would like to go to her singles-club Christmas dinner on the coming Saturday. As an afterthought, she apologized for not ringing earlier.

Penny almost choked. "Why on earth would I want to do that?"

But Julie was not easily put off.

"Because it will do you good to go out – and anyway, you'll be going as my guest."

If James and Lara hadn't been at home, Penny wouldn't have even considered the idea.

James was the first off the mark: "Mum, lighten up. Dad wouldn't have wanted you to sit at home thinking."

Then it was Lara's turn: "Mum, you have to try these things. It's all experience."

'Experience.' Penny wondered what Lara knew about experience.

However, later she gave in to the pressure, and agreed to go.

Deciding on what to wear, Penny tried on, and took off, different outfits, and every time she said, "I can't possibly go in that."

When Lara asked, "Why not?" Penny's reply was always the same: "Because I wouldn't feel comfortable in it without your father."

Finally, in exasperation, Lara said, "Mum, don't do this to yourself."

In the end she settled for a plain black dress with a flattering black patent-leather belt, her high-heeled sandals and a long fashionable gold chain. Lara said for her age she looked very elegant.

Taking this as a compliment, Penny smiled and waited for Julie to arrive.

Ten minutes later, in a cascade of colour, perfume and anticipation, she appeared. With sparkling clips in her dark hair, and silver pointed Victorian shoes, she fluttered her false eyelashes with consummate perfection.

Once inside the car, Julie rather nervously announced, "After dinner there's dancing. Do you mind?"

Sensing she felt uncomfortable, Penny said of course she didn't mind. Then, realizing how difficult she must appear, she felt guilty.

When Ben died, she had tried not to burden anyone with her sadness, and most of the time she had shed her tears when she was alone. But now she felt she had surprised everybody, and as she had unwittingly moved the boundaries they hadn't known how to cope.

Promising all the magic of Christmas, the enormous glittering Christmas tree stood proudly in the entrance of the hotel; and just in case guests failed to get the message, the inside of the foyer was decorated from floor to ceiling in dazzling silver and gold garlands. But it was the haunting strains of 'It's Going to Be a Blue Christmas Without You' that proved to be a step too far.

They looked at each other, and Julie said, "You're not bloody kidding!"

Penny laughingly replied, "Right hotel, wrong moment."

Aware that this was the first flippant remark to have passed her lips in nearly twelve months, she could see it had pleased Julie.

Julie introduced her to Donald, John, Madge and Polly. At dinner she sat beside Donald and John; and since they were both accomplished raconteurs, without even thinking she was able to return their banter.

Later, while Julie went to speak to some friends, Penny sat with Madge and Paul. Madge, with her comforting manner and matronly appearance, and Paul, small, slight and anxious to please, were such easy company she felt as though she had known them for years.

But it was the band that nearly proved her undoing. In keeping with the mood and the time of the year, they were playing all the old nostalgic torch songs. Looking at everyone enjoying themselves, Penny felt envious and resentful, and since these were emotions she had not previously been even remotely familiar with, she thought if hearts could break, that was what was happening to hers.

Trying her best to be sociable, she listened to the general chit-chat around the table, and then at the far end of the room she saw Julie. Penny watched as, in her own glorious way, she charmed and circulated with a style and panache only Julie on a roll had. Suddenly, for some unfathomable reason, her spirits lifted, and later she made herself take part in the 'fun' dances.

On the way home, Julie said, "Well, has it been a success?"
And Penny was pleased to say it had.

Every year, for as long as anyone could remember, the seating
plan for the Christmas dinner had been done by Molly, and every
year her decisions caused a mild furore. Nigel had tried in vain to
persuade her to let someone else have a go. But Molly was of the
old school – it had always been her job and she was not about to
relinquish it. The problem was, unless you objected, you sat where
it suited Molly for you to sit. Accordingly, any little disputes had to
be forgotten. Using her wisdom and the office grapevine, those not
exactly seeing eye to eye were always seated next to each other.
Most found it rather amusing and accepted it with good humour,
but some were unable to resist the temptation for a bit of tit-for-
tat. After they'd seen the plan, Molly's phone usually became a
hotline of feigned indignation.
    Exasperated by what was going on, eventually Nigel would
shout from his office, "Bloody hell, Molly – let somebody else do
it next time."
    But of course she never did.
    This morning, as she prepared to pin the plan on to the
noticeboard, Simon took a quick look and drily said, "You've done
it again, Molly. You'd better fasten your safety belt before the fun
starts."
    Molly's reaction to this was to immediately snatch the paper
from Simon, saying, "Well, you try doing it for a change."
    With a knowing smile Simon said, "If I did, I'd make it a lot
easier."
    Then with a condescending "By Saturday everybody will be
happy" Molly flounced out of the office.

In the grey swirling mist the country lanes were silent, so it was a
relief when in a blaze of coloured lights the restaurant came into
view. In true Christmas spirit, Santa's sledge ('full of hopes and
dreams' was Penny's rather fanciful thinking) looked out from an
almost unbelievable height against the dark night sky.
    Quickly parking her car, she hurried into the restaurant.

Surrounded by decorations that were almost too smart and sophisticated, an elderly silver-haired gentleman sat softly playing at the highly polished grand piano. Nearby, making all the commercial glamour pale into insignificance, the gentle innocence of the beautifully detailed Nativity scene quite simply took her breath away. And for one idyllic moment Penny's thoughts turned to Ben.

With the arrival of Nigel, her daydreaming came to an abrupt end.

He came straight over to her, and, having seen a small card on top of the piano saying 'Requests Welcomed', he mockingly bowed and asked, "What would you like to hear?"

Almost too quickly, Penny replied, "You choose."

Without hesitation he went across to the pianist, who began to play the quietly lilting strains of 'The Way We Were'. Penny wondered if she would always feel this stomach-churning sadness.

During the meal she tried not to let her feelings show, and after sharing a joke with Simon she was pleased when he said he'd just caught a glimpse of the old Penny.

Nick was still with Angela, and Simon was happy to be without any commitments, so they were both on form. Greg, always a good listener, was having his ear bent by Molly.

Now, since Molly's son was no longer at home, she was left with Albert; and because their relationship had gone rather stale, she was a little dissatisfied with life. At times she did like to be the centre of attention. This was why Penny always thought she actually enjoyed her occasional ding-dongs with Nick and Simon.

Colin was telling a few old jokes, and Beth was waiting to be with Pauline, her friend from the sales office.

But it was Dot's long dangling earrings that were the success of the night. With every slight movement of her head, they swayed at such an alarming speed they seemed to be hypnotizing Brian.

At the end of the meal, Charles Farrington said a few brief words. Then when he mischievously said now that he and Daphne were up to date with the news they could go home everyone thought that was it, and there was a sudden mass exodus to the bar.

36

Smiling, Charles Farrington sat down.

With the meal over and the dividing doors opened, there was a small area for dancing. Standing confidently by the piano, the singer (in a dress with a neckline so low the price tag could only have been based on experience) was singing an old standard. According to Simon, she was doing this with such husky-voiced sexiness her somewhat doubtful age was an irrelevance. There's no accounting for taste – Penny thought she sounded more like an engine on full throttle.

After a while, all hot and breathless, Nigel came to sit by her.

"I don't know whether it's me getting old," he said, "but enjoying yourself can be bloody hard work."

'That's true,' thought Penny.

After the frenetic pace of the last few songs, the slow ballads were being given an airing.

Nigel looked at her and said, "Come on – let's dance."

Although last week she had joined in the 'fun' dances, this somehow seemed different. Telling herself not to be silly, she meekly followed Nigel. Sensing her uncertainty, he carefully guided her around the small floor, and she thought how kind he could be. But, as Molly would say, "After all, he is a ladies' man."

As soon as the dance was over, he was off to chat up Kaye from the downstairs office, and Penny was more than content to sit with Colin and Molly. Then Nick joined them.

"Don't look now," he said, "but the new boss has just arrived."

Wearing light-coloured trousers, a black polo-neck sweater and a dark jacket, Max went to sit with his parents. Later he could be seen chatting to Sam, and then, proving he had mastered the art of extricating himself from a conversation at will, he quickly did the rounds. After he had spoken to Colin, Molly was at her regal best, and when this happened she was either right on target or she missed by a mile.

Tonight when she said, "Well, I didn't expect to see you here!" she missed by a mile.

Completely ignoring her remark, Max turned to speak to Penny. Giving the impression he was surprised to see her, he asked how things were.

Feeling awkward, she just about managed to say, "Fine, thank you."

And then she immediately thought, 'What a stupid thing to say! I'm not fine.'

His "Good" was almost a dismissal, and as he walked away she realized that communicating with Max Farrington was not going to be easy.

Around eleven thirty things were getting hectic, and, quite frankly, she had lost interest. After she'd said goodnight to anyone not too preoccupied, Nigel went with her to the car. With a quick peck on the cheek, he thanked her for listening to him.

"I really can be a miserable old sod at times."

She smiled, and said, "Only sometimes."

For the children's sake Penny tried to make Christmas happy. Surrounded by the family, she played charades and joined in the games, but she understood now why so many people dreaded this time of the year.

She missed so many things about Ben: the way they talked, the way he teased her, his tolerance when her hasty decisions backfired and, although she never realized it at the time, the gentle way he tried to prepare her for what he saw (and she hadn't) as the inevitable.

But one particular remark had been increasingly on her mind. After his first chemotherapy, he had been taken into hospital, and one day he seemed more agitated than usual.

After a while he tried to sit up in bed, and as she went to help he whispered, "Penny, if I have to leave you, promise you'll try and make somebody else happy."

Completely shocked, she could hardly speak, but when she looked at his earnest face she just about managed to nod her head in agreement, and it was never mentioned again.

Knowing she had pleased him was all that mattered, because, whatever happened (and that was something she didn't even dare to think about), she knew there could never be another Ben.

But she had to be honest and admit some things were getting

easier. When she was doing something that had been Ben's job she didn't always become tearful and cry, but it remained a mystery why some things got no easier at all. For instance, still at the top of her list of situations best avoided was laughing alone, and worse still would be watching a sentimental film. Both seemed such joyless experiences – the mere thought sent shivers down her spine.

Thoroughly enjoying the disruption they were causing, Simon and Nick were taking down the Christmas decorations, and Dot with her hair swept into one of her formidable buns was issuing her instructions: "Careful, Simon! Oh, Nick, you're going to break that."

With tinsel and streamers falling like confetti, and balloons floating around the office, without a care in the world Molly (oblivious to the chaos around her) sat looking at the paperwork on her desk.

The garage was back to normal in a few days, though the clerical staff had ten days' holiday. Nigel came in to attend to any urgent post, but the rest he left for Molly.

She complained that "Every year this happens, and it just isn't good enough."

Nick, with remarkable accuracy, was dropping a small silver star right into the middle of Dot's outlandish bun, and as she gave out a loud scream Max Farrington, with perfect timing, appeared.

With an icy "Good morning" he walked quickly to his office and, before anyone could answer, the door closed with a mighty thud.

Nigel, who had been in the showroom for the last half-hour, arrived just in time to witness the scene.

Absolutely furious, he almost snarled, "Well, thanks a lot! That's a bloody good start."

Needless to say, the rest of the decorations were quietly taken down, and, in a suitably orderly fashion, were put into their boxes until next year.

With a lot of news to catch up on, everyone stayed in at lunchtime.

Nigel looked as though he was going to work through his break, but because he hadn't spoken since his early morning outburst no one was quite sure. Dot idly rearranged the food around her plate. She seemed to be distracted.

Then as Nigel passed her desk he suddenly said, "Seen Brian over Christmas?"

Dot's quiet "Yes" left everyone stunned.

Obviously still feeling rather disgruntled, his voice was full of sarcasm as he asked, "And how many years has it taken you to do that?"

Looking decidedly uneasy, Dot's "Too many" sounded almost sad.

With Nigel having effectively put paid to any further questions, there was an embarrassed silence.

Seizing the opportunity to change the subject, Nick with a pronounced stutter (always an ominous sign) hesitantly said, "Well, I don't know if it's the right time to tell you, with Dot and everything, but" – and he cleared his throat – "I'm getting married."

"Married!" Simon almost choked. "Who to?"

Looking really hurt, Nick said, "Angela, of course."

"Whatever for?"

"Simon," Penny admonished, "don't be so unkind."

"I'm sorry, but why on earth would anyone want to get married?"

"Don't be silly," Molly piped up. "Haven't you noticed, people do get married?"

"Not me," Simon retorted.

Ignoring that remark, Nick said, "You're all invited to the evening do."

With the wedding arranged for the weekend before Easter, Nick said Angela's three children (Brian had been right – Olivia, twelve; Vicky, ten; and Josh, seven) were nearly as excited as himself. A few years older than Nick, Angela sounded far more experienced, but, since Nick could be unbelievably immature, Dot thought this might be a good thing. When everybody wanted to know what she was like, Nick needed no prompting.

"W-e-ll, she's got long blonde hair, she's pretty, and in a way I suppose she looks quite delicate." And then, making it sound like an apology, he added, "And she makes me laugh."

Unable to stop herself, Molly, with all the cynicism of the disappointed, said, "Well, if you're prepared to work at it . . ." And her voice trailed away.

Simon was clearly frustrated at the pedestrian course the conversation was taking, and in a moment of pure inspiration he decided to bring it to a level he was more used to communicating on: "Let's cut to the chase, Nick: is she good in bed?"

Molly nearly fell off her chair. Then with a sweeping exaggerated gesture she put her hands over her ears, and in a horrified tone of voice said, "We don't want to know that, Simon."

Now, at this point something of the old fun-loving Penny surfaced and she calmly said, "Well, perhaps some of us do, Molly."

Molly looked at her and could barely conceal her disapproval. Her prim "I'm surprised at you, Penny!" sounded almost like a reprimand.

Penny smiled and said, "Only joking."

Since Molly was secretly pleased to see some of Penny's humour returning, she gently smiled and said, "I should think so too."

Suspecting he was missing something, Nigel came to stand by Penny's desk.

Turning to look at her, he lifted his eyebrows and with a glint of approval he quietly said, "Good for you."

With lunchtime nearly over, Beth felt rather put out because the Christmas-dinner shenanigans hadn't been mentioned.

One year without Ben, and sometimes Penny felt it was only yesterday; but if she was honest, it was beginning to feel like another lifetime. Throughout all the sadness there wasn't much she could clearly remember. If she thought things might suddenly get better, of course they didn't, but nowadays she no longer received a constant stream of advice. Life had moved on, but for Penny time seemed to have stood still.

Shortly before Christmas Julie convinced her that joining her psychology class might help.

41

Tonight she was looking forward to her first class. Although she didn't know what to expect, she suspected with Julie the evening wouldn't be dull.

When she arrived, she looked for all the world as though she was about to begin an Arctic expedition. Now, admittedly, earlier in the day there had been a light snowfall, but with her thick brightly patterned coat, woollen hat, high boots, and the scarf she had wrapped so many times around her neck she was in danger of decapitating herself, she proved once again she was the master of the exotic.

The stark grandeur of the austere Victorian buildings surrounding the modern college usually made them seem like silent bastions, but today, with the pure-white snow nestling in every nook and cranny, they looked a picture of comforting timeless perfection.

With his long frizzy brown hair pulled tightly back into a ponytail, Marcus (the tutor, and somewhere in his late thirties) sat patiently on the corner of his desk and greeted everyone with a warm, pleasant smile.

With about half a dozen new people, he asked everyone to introduce themselves, and then to briefly say their reasons for joining the class. There were two solicitors, quite a number of social workers, a young man training to be a criminal psychologist, three nuns and a few young people hoping to advance their careers.

Marcus's illustrated talk on body language was interrupted by one perceptive question after another, and his knowledgeable answers were amusing and interesting. After giving examples of how in our posture, mannerisms and eye contact we innocently give away a lot about ourselves, he proceeded to put it to the test. Moving from one person to another, he identified with remarkable accuracy (so he was told) many traits in their personalities that were not immediately obvious. He pointed out that some people had a natural empathy for others, and he said it was possible for us to learn how to develop empathy in ourselves. This was interesting. Under different circumstances you could have been forgiven for thinking he was some sort of clairvoyant, or at the very least that he had psychic powers.

After the break, Marcus said each week he expected an essay to be written on whatever topic had been discussed. Penny didn't mind at all – in fact she was looking forward to stimulating her thinking powers again.

Choosing the subject of romantic love, Marcus read an extract from the book he had in front of him, and Penny thought the writer sounded pretty cynical. When he finished reading, Marcus asked for the students' thoughts on the subject. But no one was forthcoming.

He persevered: "Come on – some of you must have your own ideas."

Still there was silence.

Penny thought the young ones looked subdued, and, since the class were usually eager to voice their opinions, Julie found their reluctance strange.

Then suddenly, without really thinking, Penny said, "Of course it's possible."

With everybody looking towards her, Marcus asked, "It's Penny, isn't it?"

She said it was.

Then they all wanted to know how she knew.

Almost losing her nerve, she wanted to crawl under the table, but instead she boldly said, "Well, it's like Santa Claus really – it brings a bit of magic."

With remarkable good humour, Marcus said, "Would you like to take this part of the lesson, Penny?"

Smiling, she shook her head. "No, thank you."

But it had done the trick, and soon views were being bounced around like ping-pong balls.

Throughout all this, Julie was so dumbfounded she appeared lost for words, and on the way home she said she couldn't get over how Penny had got herself so involved. Since it was the first time she had done something and not been reminded of Ben, Penny was just as surprised as Julie. It also challenged her comfortable conviction that without Ben she would never be interested in anything again. This made Penny think about the many wise words she had heard at the bereavement group.

After six months with the group, Penny decided it was time to put all the help she had received into practice.

Hillary and Phil said they understood, and Patsy and Ethel said although they were going to miss her they were pleased she felt ready to slowly move on.

Penny had always been touched by the interest they had shown her. By the same token, just listening to them share their hard-earned pearls of wisdom was something Penny would never forget; and not wanting to lose their friendship, she regularly phoned them.

Today, Penny was to have her first monthly meeting with Max Farrington. For more years than she cared to remember, these meetings had taken place with Charles Farrington, and after going through the accounts she had always looked forward to their little chats, but somehow she didn't think an *informal* chat would be on Max Farrington's agenda.

When he eventually asked her to come into his office, it seemed strange to see him sitting in the chair his father had always occupied. This morning, in his dark woollen suit, white shirt and tasteful blue tie, he looked every inch the successful businessman. Penny thought there was a delicacy about his well-groomed hands and immaculate fingernails that was somehow out of keeping with this rather stern-looking man. But it was his eyes she found the most disturbing. The pupils seemed almost unnaturally dilated, and they appeared unseeing and without emotion. Penny found their emptiness almost frightening.

"Are you ready to start?"

Max Farrington's words brought her quickly down to earth, making her feel gauche and nervous.

"Eh, yes," she stammered.

She already found herself resenting him.

Starting to go through the accounts, he spoke so quietly she frequently had to ask, "Pardon?"

When he came to the end of the first page nothing happened, and Penny wondered if there was a problem.

Then, breaking the silence like the clear-cut crack of an iceberg, he coldly said, "Next."

Now Penny didn't quite know what was expected of her, and she sat like a ten-year-old waiting for his instructions.

With none forthcoming, she timidly said, "It's on the next page."

In a voice that sounded as though he didn't quite know whether to humour or patronize her, his "Yes" hung in the air like a question mark.

Suddenly she realized he actually expected her to turn the page over for him. What was wrong with the man? She didn't think even his apprentices would have pandered to his whims in this way. With this thought, some of her old fire returned, and she whipped the page over with such force she nearly tore it from end to end.

With a look she couldn't quite fathom, he seemed to be rather put out at her reaction.

'Good,' she thought, 'because I'm certainly not going to do that every time.'

But it was no contest. Although it was such a trivial matter, Penny felt he was making it clear where the boundaries lay, and he had no intention of moving any goalposts.

Trying to be reasonable, Penny understood that since this was the first time he had seen the detailed accounts, he was naturally going to ask a lot of questions. She was pleased he seemed satisfied with her answers. But she was also becoming aware that although his father had trusted her judgements, his son was going to do no such thing. Listening to the decisions he made, she thought there was a certain ruthlessness about him.

Finally, after making sure she had all the necessary notes, he handed back the accounts, and with a curt "Thanks" he indicated the meeting was over.

Since Penny never took into consideration the fact that at least once a week the traffic was so slow it literally ground to a halt, she was often late for work, and this morning was no exception. (To be fair, on the days this happened she never took her full lunch break, but it was a glaring example of how stubborn she could be.) Ben used to say she only stayed with Farrington's because she had most of her own way, and then with a twinkle in his eye he would tease her, saying she was far too militant.

In those days Penny had to admit she had been rather vocal about anything she deemed to be an injustice, but all that seemed a long time ago. Nowadays, although a small spark might occasionally surface, most of the time she just let things wash over her.

When she walked into the office, there was a distinct air of excitement. Dot immediately came over to Penny's desk. Today, with her bohemian look a thing of the past, and her hair free from the restriction of her redoubtable bun, she was wearing a straight skirt, and underneath her short jacket Penny could see a pretty pink blouse. She proudly produced her left hand for inspection, and Penny found herself looking at a small cluster of diamonds.

Bubbling over with pride, she said, "We got engaged on Saturday."

Hugging Dot, Penny was reminded of all the years that had gone into arriving at this moment, and her thoughts instinctively turned to Ben.

That was until she heard Nigel's "Bloody hell, Dot – that was fast work!" And then: "Well, perhaps not."

A while later Brian appeared, and this was a Brian no one had ever seen before. Rejuvenated and confident, he stood protectively by Dot's side, and it nearly all became too much for Penny.

No doubt remembering his own painful memories, Nigel came over to her desk and tried to reassure her: "Come on – you had it once, and I thought I did too. Let's join the others and then it's back to work."

With everyone around Dot's desk, Max Farrington walked in.

Nick, who was still in Utopia about his own recent triumph, said, "Dot and Brian have got engaged, Max."

Surprising everybody, Max went over to Dot and asked to see her ring. In a moment that seemed formal and old-fashioned, and yet one Penny found extremely touching, he shook Brian's hand and, with a sincerity that was undeniable, he looked at them both and quietly said, "A wise choice! Congratulations. I'm very pleased."

Then, clearly feeling nothing more was expected of him, he disappeared into his office.

Spontaneity was a side of Max Farrington he normally kept well hidden. Penny wondered why he found it necessary to suppress this gentle side of his nature.

Breaking into her thoughts, Nigel turned to her and said, "I just saw his father in Max. Did you?"

And Penny agreed.

Simon, who by now was recovering from the shock, had a glint in his eye that Molly had already detected.

Before he could say a word, she said, "Don't even think about it, Simon."

Thereupon Simon innocently asked, "Think about what, Molly?"

"Don't you dare to bring sex into it" was Molly's rather direct answer.

This amused Nigel, and he couldn't resist winding her up: "What the hell's it all about, then, Molly?"

"Friendship and companionship."

And with a look that was rather suspect, she swept past him, opened a filing-cabinet drawer and said no more.

Understandably, Dot could only talk about Brian. Since they both lived with their widowed mothers, their plans at the moment were, to say the least, vague.

Nick, who in the last couple of months had matured remarkably quickly, said, "There's no rush, Dot. Now you've come this far, I'm sure you'll work something out."

Since it didn't take long for Dot and Brian's good news to reach the other departments, soon the accounts office was besieged by people all wanting to sort out their queries.

By three o'clock Nigel was beginning to feel the strain; so when Tony made his annual visit prematurely, it appeared to be the final straw.

Without looking up from his desk, he said, "Come to see Dot, Tony?"

With this Tony looked slightly uneasy.

Aware he'd been unnecessarily abrupt, Nigel tried to make

amends: "Things OK in the paint shop?"

Now, immediately the words passed his lips, Nigel knew he had made a mistake, but it was too late. With Dot temporarily forgotten, and with a vengeance only the dedicated can achieve, Tony proceeded to bend Nigel's ear.

But today's visitors brought one small snippet of gossip. The garage's petrol pumps were mainly used for demonstration cars and senior staff; and according to Barrington Clarke (who officially retired some years ago, but still enjoyed working for a few hours at the weekend), when Max Farrington called in he was always with an attractive female.

Beth took this opportunity to inform everyone that the girls downstairs found him really dishy, whereupon Molly said she was not in the least bit surprised.

Choosing to ignore the unmistakable grey streaks in his hair, she spoke with all the knowledge of the worldly-wise: "It's a well-known fact women find dark mysterious looks irresistible. It's a challenge." Then in answer to Nick's "Crumbs, Molly, you're not one of those agony aunts on the quiet, are you?" Molly got up from behind her desk, and, giving Nick one of her haughty looks, she said, "Don't be so silly."

Then she walked towards Max's office, knocked on the door and went inside.

Colin and Greg had taken all the excitement in their stride, but after the required congratulations, and Dot's insistence they take a serious look at her ring, they were soon back at their desks.

Colin was a good office intermediary and Greg was always helpful, but they did prefer to keep their heads down and just get on with things.

Penny and Heather had met some years ago, and then quite simply lost touch. When (through a mutual friend) she heard of Ben's death, Heather had written to Penny and since then they had met for coffee once a month. Small and plump, Heather's stylishly cut hair was rather too short to be considered feminine, but she was down to earth and caring, and Penny enjoyed her company.

A few weeks ago, with Heather's friends, Miriam and Ruth,

they had decided to spend a weekend in the Lake District. Like Heather, they were nurses at the local hospital, and when Penny had first met them the word 'capable' had come into her mind. Ordinary in height and build they might have been, but their flawless complexions would have put a beauty salon out of business. Heather said their healthy looks were probably due to the long treks they took with their walking club.

The day they set off was bitterly cold. Although the dark menacing clouds hovered, Heather was not one to be put off by the weather.

Sprawling long and low at the top of the village high street, the grey stone picturesque hotel had once been a coaching inn. Inside, the cluttered cosiness was instantly appealing. The walls were all decorated with a century or more of accumulated photographs and memorabilia, with a brief history by the side of each fading sepia photograph. It was an evocative look at village life over 150 years ago. The inn was a favourite stop (so it was said) for people travelling from the North to London, and it is a chastening thought that in those days even a trouble-free journey would take days.

The heavy oak furniture, blue and maroon plaid carpets and enormous sofas and armchairs had obviously seen better days, but they managed to exude an air of bygone gentility.

A few hours after the friends' arrival, no one was particularly surprised to see it had started to snow. Soon an eerie silence was beginning to descend, and with extraordinary speed everywhere was becoming virtually impassable. The hotel staff said they couldn't remember the last time this had happened.

With most of the residents now warmly ensconced in the hotel lounge, they greeted the news with remarkable fortitude. Inconveniences were soon forgotten, and the heavy snowfall brought an almost childlike excitement. Since everyone was in the same situation, inhibitions were quickly dispensed with, and a unanimous decision was taken (and eagerly agreed to by the people on their own) that since any planned walks for tomorrow would have to be cancelled, a walk around the village might be fun.

In the dining room the excitement continued, and in the adrenalin-filled atmosphere the snow was the only topic of conversation.

"Is it still snowing?"

"You can't see a thing – it's a real blizzard."

Now, all this could make you think snow had never been seen there before. It certainly seemed to be unprecedented (as the staff pointed out) at this time of the year and with such unexpected ferocity. If it had occurred before, then it must have been a very long time ago.

The menu had enough variety to satisfy all tastes. The starter of thick vegetable soup, pâté or melon was followed by a choice of fish, beef, lamb or pork, and there was a delicious sweet trolley, including hot puddings straight from the kitchen.

In the lounge board games were played, and then, later, quite a few people, including Miriam and Penny, sat around discussing a variety of contentious subjects.

The next morning the weather was fine and bright, and with thick socks, boots and numerous layers of warm clothing everyone (with much hilarity) set off to walk down to the village. Carefully putting one foot and then the other into the soft feathery snow, the more confident were soon forging ahead, avoiding snowdrifts so high they were in danger of disappearing. Every so often a powdery fluffy ball of snow found its target.

Children, adults and a couple of dozen teenagers were all pulling their sledges up a steep incline, and it wasn't long before they were seen holding on for grim life as, with more luck than judgement, they arrived safely at the bottom of the hill. There was a festive air in the village.

Penny and the others were told it would be foolish to try and walk any further, so for the rest of the morning they got into the spirit of the occasion and just entered into the fun.

Back at the hotel they had a sandwich lunch, and then Heather and Ruth put their feet up and read the books they had brought with them. Miriam and Penny made themselves comfortable and had a chat.

With just the one unmarried son, living abroad, since her divorce Miriam had been on her own. She said finding out her ex-husband was starting a new life with someone else had been as painful as the day he left her. At the time, she found a lot of their friends soon distanced themselves, and she didn't know whether this was through embarrassment or because in some way it had upset the balance of these friendships, but she had clung to those who stayed around. Although they had been kind, their company was a constant reminder of how things used to be. So when Heather and Ruth (who had never married) asked if she would like to join some of their social activities, she had jumped at the chance.

Listening to Miriam, Penny realized there are many kinds of bereavement. She thought watching someone you still love making a new life for themselves was in its own way as devastating as death in all its finality.

That evening, sitting quietly around the huge log fire, they all reflected on the last twenty-four hours, and Patrick (who should have been the leader on one of the walks) said he felt an old villager had aptly summed up the weekend.

Telling him about the cancelled itineraries, he had said, "Bugger all that! I'll bet you're enjoying this better than any itinerary."

Patrick was sure that everyone would agree.

They did, but they also said this was largely due to the fact they had all got on so well. If they hadn't, then it might have been a very different story.

That night, thinking about Miriam, Penny realized the difference between the bitterness of rejection and being with someone you love until the end was the sobering difference Miriam had found too difficult to put into words.

When Sam stood in the middle of the office, it was always a sign he had some important news to get off his chest. Since he knew everything, he probably knew Max wasn't in today.

After clearing his throat, he said, "You'll never guess what I've been doing this weekend."

"I hope it's nothing that's going to upset Molly" was Nick's quick reply.

Ignoring this, Molly said, "Well, go on, then – tell us."

"I've been working on the cottage Max has just bought."

Now, since Sam could turn his hand to anything, there was nothing unusual about that. But Max Farrington buying a cottage – now, that was news.

"Where?" everybody wanted to know.

"In the village next to his father's at Krayton."

This was a pretty little village about eight miles away.

The next question had to be "What's it like?"

After giving this some considerable thought, he carefully answered, "Well, just let's say when all the work is finished it'll be the best in the village."

"There's only about a dozen cottages in the place" was Greg's rather surly comment.

"Well," said Sam, sounding a trifle miffed, "it'll still be the best."

"With his money, I'm not surprised."

Clearly it was not one of Greg's better days.

Simon, as usual, was quick to have his say: "Well, with all the women he's supposed to have, he's got to take them somewhere. He can hardly live with his parents."

"That", said Sam, "was always going to be a temporary measure. A man like that doesn't live with his parents for long."

"All the same, I'll bet it's cramped his style" was Nick's contribution.

The subject of Max Farrington's love life was an endless source of interest to the female members of staff, and Simon pointed this out.

Sam replied with a withering "Well, I don't know why they bother. He's not going to look at anyone at Farrington's, now, is he?"

But Molly was quick to point out, "His father did."

Nowadays, there was only Sam and Frank who could remember, but the story was legendary. Sam, however, seemed to have forgotten how over the years it had been passed down through the staff, and each time it was told it grew ever more romantic.

It seems when he first took over from his father he inherited Joan, the company secretary; and when she retired, Daphne came in her place. According to the version Charles liked to tell, he knew from the moment Daphne walked into his office that she was going to be 'the one'.

Sam said he remembered it well. "She was a lovely girl. He couldn't have done better."

"In that case," Simon said, "who knows – one day history might repeat itself!"

"I doubt it" was Sam's rather scathing reply.

Seeing he was enjoying all the nostalgia, Simon thought he'd keep things going: "Now, why do you doubt that, Sam?"

"Because at his age I wouldn't think he'd bother getting married. And if he does it'll be somebody either all snooty and uppity, or some dolly bird."

This incensed Molly: "I think you're forgetting the type of person he is, Sam. From what I've seen, I don't think he'd go for the snooty or dolly-bird types." Then, seeing Simon's raised eyebrows, she hurriedly added, "Well, he might take them out, but, you mark my words, if he does marry it will be to someone warm and funny, and by then he'll have lost that remote way of his."

"Well, maybe." Then, after asking if anyone had seen Nigel (and they hadn't), Sam said he would be back later.

Simon, who never could resist teasing Molly, said, "I wish I knew so much about people, Molly. I'll bet I'd have found somebody by now."

"I thought finding somebody was the last thing you wanted to do, Simon."

Nick's "I like that one, Molly" was totally ignored.

With that, Beth looked across at Penny and asked, "Do you think Max will get married, Penny?"

Since she doubted at this stage he ever would, she said, "Well, if he does, I don't think he'll be very easy to live with."

"I know, and it's such a shame!" Beth's rather amusing reply ended the matter.

When Nigel appeared, Max's cottage was being discussed. Sensing he had missed something, Molly took it upon herself to tell him Sam's news.

Penny was the first to admit Charles Farrington would always be a hard act to follow, but this morning, after her third monthly meeting with Max, things hadn't improved. He had none of his father's easy charm; and although Dot and Molly said when they went in to see him he was always helpful, this never happened with Penny. She was still the one to turn the pages of the customers' accounts, and every month she vowed it was going to be the last time. Maybe it was just unfortunate, but she found him so cold and disapproving she felt unable to be natural in his company.

With Nick's wedding only a week away, everyone in the office had been invited. He went to considerable trouble to explain why he'd not been able to invite anyone from the other offices. The evening reception was being held in the local village hall, and, since it was not a large room, after family and friends had been invited they had no option but to limit the rest of the invitations.

Having said that, the other day after spending most of the morning with Max he had on impulse invited him along.

"Is he coming?" everybody wanted to know.

"Well, he's promised if he can he'll pop in later in the evening."

Penny hoped it would be later, but Dot went all dewy-eyed at the prospect.

Every morning for the last week, Nick had issued a bulletin on the progress of his wedding arrangements. This led Colin and Greg to say they knew more about Nick's wedding plans than they ever had about their own.

Even Beth, who at first had been thrilled, said, "If getting married takes all this planning, I don't think I'll bother,"

Nigel, on hearing that Angela's dress was a secret, felt compelled to say, "Well, that's about the only bloody thing that is."

With Dot and Molly, Penny went to see them get married. Inside the registry office, the pink wallpaper, elaborate chandeliers and vases of freshly cut flowers all helped to make the room look pleasant and inviting. The registrar (who unfortunately had all the charisma of an undertaker) stood behind a long, dark wooden table.

Nick in a smart grey suit was looking tense and nervous seated on the front row, but as soon as Angela arrived he visibly relaxed. She was wearing a flattering cream dress and matching jacket, both her daughters were in blue, and Josh looked very grown-up in his dark-blue jacket and long trousers.

For the short ceremony, the registrar (obviously a real trooper) changed his persona into an agreeable smiling contradiction of his former self.

Knowing how much Nick had wanted this, Penny, Dot and Molly all shed a few tears.

Penny had a preference for high necklines – the depth to which they plunged was (in her eyes) a crucial giveaway regarding someone's confidence. This perhaps tells you more about Penny than she would have liked you to know. The multicoloured dress she was wearing with the neckline that had given her so much angst (the bewildered sales assistant couldn't understand such concern for the propriety of a neckline which in her opinion wasn't even low) was the catalyst that made Penny determined to do something about herself.

And do something she did. Slowly she began to change. And one day she would come to realize that nature had also given her a helping hand.

To her friends, the change was becoming very clear. Gradually they noticed a lot of her old indecision had gone. Now if they asked her to join them, she generally did. Quite simply, she was beginning to regain her confidence.

Adding her favourite slingback sandals, she was ready to pick up Molly, who for reasons best known to herself was not coming with Albert. She had also promised to pick up Beth, but unfortunately

Beth had a nasty cold and said she couldn't possibly come with a red nose! Colin and Greg would be with their wives. If the past was anything to go by, they would only socialize amongst themselves.

Inside the village hall, Nick's mum and sister had decorated the room with streamers and banners, all proudly announcing 'Just Married'.

Simon had just arrived. Seeing Nigel with Dot and Brian, he went to sit by them.

During the buffet, Colin and Greg chatted to everybody, but as soon as the dancing began they went back to their own table.

When it was announced the next ten minutes would be 'Rock-and-Roll Time', Simon looked at Penny and said, "Come on – let's give it a go."

Since it looked like being fun, they all trooped on to the dance floor, and soon Penny was following Simon's hip-jerking, body-swaying movements with a sense of fun she hadn't felt for a very long time.

Afterwards, on the way back to their table, she suddenly tripped, and after trying to regain her balance she looked up into the cold eyes of Max Farrington. If the floor had swallowed her up, that would have been fine, but, hoping he'd arrived too late to have seen her dancing, she salvaged as much dignity as she could and sat down.

Casually dressed, he had taken off his jacket to reveal a green-and-white checked shirt, and Penny thought the soft kid shoes he wore would probably have cost her a week's salary.

When Nick with his parents (and it seemed his entire family) came to have a word, Max Farrington, simply doing what was expected of him (and if he chose to, he could obviously do it rather well), showed his ingenuous charm to the full. But to the observant onlooker this disciplined man had a detachment that implied a deep emotional involvement (for him) would be the ultimate commitment.

Immediately Nick and his 'entourage' had moved to another table, he turned to Brian and asked, "Do you mind if I dance with Dot, Brian?"

Now, for Brian to be consulted on such a matter was an entirely new experience. By the look on his face, the polite recognition of the status that up until now Dot had denied him left him feeling quite overwhelmed by it all.

After a long silence, he just about managed to say, "Of course not."

Turning to Penny, Molly quietly said, "We'll never hear the last of this one."

But it didn't take long before it was Molly's turn, and later, still glowing from the aftermath of his attention, she said, "When are you going to ask Penny to dance, Max?"

Giving Penny a meaningful look that spoke volumes, he said, "I think Penny dances rather too well for me."

So he had seen her!

It didn't help matters when Dot quickly pointed out, "You dance really well, Max."

Thankfully, Nigel spared her any further embarrassment: "Come on, Penny – let's see if I can keep up with you."

Since he was an exceptionally good dancer, and Penny knew she wasn't, she thought how kind he could be. But when she felt Nigel holding her a little too closely, she gently moved away, and she just hoped Max Farrington hadn't noticed.

It was only later she thought, 'Did it really matter if he had?'

When Nick eventually appeared with Angela, it was congratulations all round. Penny noticed before he said a word Max quickly rose to his feet, and she grudgingly had to admit he was in many ways like his father.

By midnight things were clearly getting boisterous, and, after having a word with Nick, Max said goodnight. Soon everybody else was doing the same.

In his own inimitable way, Nigel said, "Well, folks, it's been a bloody good night."

Penny had helped with the cricket teas since James and Lara were toddlers, and afterwards, if Daddy had been bowling, they would scream with delight.

When James began to play for the club, it was said for a young fast bowler he was remarkably accurate, and his ability to take wickets for minimal runs gave him a healthy bowling average.

When Ben no longer played, he went to watch James, and he always looked forward to his spell of bowling. Building up speed like an oncoming tornado, his arrival at the crease was like the climax of a storm. Then he let rip with an overarm action so powerful that the ball went hurtling towards the batsman with alarming ferocity.

But this season had been dismal. Without the support and guidance of his father, no matter how hard he tried, he just couldn't find his form. When he had been dropped from the first team he remembered how it had thrilled his father to see him open the first team's bowling, and his confidence now hit an all-time low. This made him realize he needed to do something about things, and he decided that before he went back to university he would speak to the club's committee.

Since only retired players of the club were eligible to join this elite band (and apart from complying with the demands of the cricket league they had no other outside influences), nothing much ever changed. They were not a wealthy club, so any expensive renovations could quite easily have seen their rapid demise. Their dislike of change may have been just sensible logic – a consequence of their dire financial situation. For as long as anyone could remember, they had met in an upstairs room at the local pub, and from all accounts everything was taken very seriously. Although humour may have been in short supply, it was said their caustic wit would have been a comedian's dream.

It was hardly surprising, then, that the uninitiated, attending for the first time, found the hierarchy reigned supreme. They soon got the message that to question any of their decisions would be tantamount to treason. To avoid this ordeal, the players usually sorted out their own little differences, but on the rare occasions anyone did request to see the committee he generally came away with an amusing tale to tell.

There was one favourite story about a young player who, during a spell of unseasonable weather, had (for three Saturdays in a row) been sent to bowl 'up-bank' against the wind. Considering this to be unfair, he had asked to see a committee member. Thereupon, the story goes, he was told, "We're not God, lad. We can't do anything about the weather!"

And that, it appeared, had been that.

During the winter, they met once a month, but in the cricket season, along with the club's captain, they met each week. First to be discussed would be the previous Saturday's game. A player's success would be applauded, and any lack of success would sometimes be gone over in the most intimate detail. This would be followed by the all-important batting order for the coming Saturday. With a thoroughness that would have put a psychiatrist to shame, each player's skill, temperament and stamina was analysed.

Who should open the bowling was always a problem – fast, slow or medium pace? And since the weather and the state of the pitch would ultimately determine their tactics, they took all the likelihoods into consideration, then drew up a list that was a masterpiece of contradictions.

Before James had his meeting, Penny decided his decision to leave the club meant it was the right time for her to do the same. Langdale held too many memories, and during the last year she had always come home longing for how it used to be. She thought about the day Ben got his hat-trick, and the time he decimated a team and got eight wickets for only a few runs, the afternoons his bowling was knocked all over the ground, and the infamous occasion he allowed a batsman to hit him for four consecutive sixes, and now Penny found little comfort in remembering.

Although she had felt she was letting them down, everybody understood her reasons. But they did tease her, and someone said what about the profits from her cakes?

(Before a home game, she had always baked four large sponge cakes, and, since they were popular, it was all a bit of extra money for the club.)

Then they reminded her of the time a visiting player had walked into the pavilion and shouted, "Save us some of your cake, Mrs Hathaway."

It was only a small room, and it got shabbier each year, but it was doubtful if any of the people in it that night would have noticed. To their knowledge, no one else ever used it, and it didn't concern them at all that there was little furniture, or the walls that had once been a pleasant cream colour were now a sickly brown. They had high-backed comfortable chairs and a long wooden table, and this was sufficient for their needs. Since the club never paid for the privilege, it was an ideal arrangement.

They met at their usual time of seven thirty, and this gave them half an hour in which to collect their thoughts before seeing James.

During the summer, they all commented on how he had grown uncannily like his father. They were well aware of why he was coming to see them, and for their oldest member it brought back a memory of another night, when Ben as a young player had walked into this room hoping to be chosen to play for Langdale. Now, all these years later, and for a very different reason, his son (not much younger than his father had been at the time) was about to sit at this table, and the poignancy of the situation made him conscious of his own advancing years.

James walked up the stairs of the ancient-looking Barnacle Arms, and felt relieved he was about to get things off his chest.

When he knocked on the door at the end of the landing, a voice boomed, "Come in."

Inside, the eight or nine people sitting around the table beckoned him to come and sit with them.

After a warm welcome, he was anxious to get started, and without any interruptions he had his say.

When he had finally said it all, he heard someone clear his throat and mumble, "Too many memories."

Then, during a long chat, they made it clear they felt he was making the right decision. Thanking him for his efforts, and wishing him well, they said how much he was going to be missed.

Now came a brisk "Time to move on, James."

At the beginning of the evening, they had decided there would be no long inquest and no pressure put on him to stay. Without any more preamble, they set about helping him.

When he said he liked the idea of joining the village team

at Asher (he knew some of the players, and as a member of a visiting team he had played on their ground), they all said, "Good choice, lad! Your father always had a lot of time for that club."

James didn't want to be reminded, but he knew they were only trying to be helpful. They seemed pleased to tell him that Asher had good practising facilities and the best professional advice, and in the past one of their players had been selected to play for the county.

Later he listened to them reminiscing, and although they were careful not to mention his father's name it still made him realize how much he was missing him.

Anxious to get away, he said he really must leave, and after thanking them he left.

Outside, all his hurt, anger and frustration was in the almighty kick that dented his car door, and he thought, '- - - -!'

With rows of thatched ivy-clad cottages and colourful gardens, Asher village had won the 'Best Kept Village' prize for two consecutive years. There was an abundance of signs to this effect, so it was obviously not something they intended to keep to themselves.

The Ranton was the village pub, and it was here James had agreed to meet Jacob West.

After parking his car, he heard someone ask, "James Hathaway?"

Turning around, he found himself looking at a man in his early fifties, tall, balding and as slim as himself. Then, with outstretched hand, he introduced himself.

"Jacob West. Pleased to meet you, James."

Once inside the Ranton they sat in the corner by the old stone fireplace, surrounded by brass ornaments, pictures of hunting scenes and a large blackboard that still had scrawled in chalk the names and score from the previous night's darts match. There was a comfortable and friendly atmosphere.

Although Jacob appeared precise and serious, James found him likeable. He had an amazing knowledge of the club's history, and he was interesting company. He said there was plenty of good-natured rivalry to be selected for Asher's first team, and no one ever missed (unless with good reason) the Tuesday-night net practice.

Later, when the conversation turned to his father, James was surprised to find how well Jacob had known him. He listened to one or two amusing stories he hadn't heard before. Jacob had been interested to hear about his mother; and when James said she would no longer be helping with the teas at Langdale, he nodded sympathetically. It seemed to have touched a raw nerve.

With what sounded like a hopeless sigh he said, "Nowadays the tea rotas are left to the faithful few." Then suddenly, turning to James, he asked, "Do you think your mother would be interested in helping out at Asher?"

With all the confidence of youth, James didn't hesitate: "I'll bet she would."

Immediately Jacob found a scrap of paper and hurriedly wrote down a couple of names and phone numbers, and asked if nearer the time Penny would give one of them a ring, adding that before the start of the next season he would be in touch with James.

When it was time to leave, James had the strange feeling his decision to come to Asher might not have been entirely his own. He could almost hear his father saying, "It's all in that little book!"

Over the holidays, when their friends came round, James and Lara had noticed that the chaos no longer drove their mother mad. In fact she seemed to revel in it.

"Mum, you're different" was all they kept saying, and Penny knew it was true.

Now the shambolic state of the house didn't upset her; now she saw it as alive and lived in, and deep down she knew the difference was just the wisdom of hindsight.

Since it was a big rambling house, it had always been a haven for James and Lara's friends, and the phone and doorbell appeared to be in constant use. When Ben died and the children went away, the change had been sudden and drastic.

On her own, Penny went around finding fault with the place, but with the arrival of visitors all her anxieties disappeared.

With James looking forward to his cricket, and the summer job he had found for himself in one of the bookshops in town, things were looking up. Lara (with a little help from Heather) was going to help on the reception desk at the hospital, and according to Lara she just couldn't wait.

At the moment Lara couldn't wait for anything, and sometimes Penny was reminded of herself at Lara's age. Inevitably there were moments when their personalities well and truly clashed. The question of time was particularly frustrating: there was time, and then there was Lara's time.

For instance, in answer to any request, it was always "In a minute, Mum." And since this required a rethink on the definition of a minute, Penny usually blew her top.

Before he went back to university, James had reminded Penny to speak to somebody about the teas at Asher. Remembering how James had walked into the house that night and said he had promised Jacob West she would help with teas, she could hardly believe it was over eight months ago. At the time she had felt quite annoyed; but since September she had changed, and now she was looking forward to meeting new people.

When she rang Maisie Pepadine, she had been so pleased to hear that Penny was happy to go on to their tea rota that Penny found herself agreeing to be there for the next home game.

At the end of the month it was always busy at work, and for most days this week everyone had kept their heads down.

This morning Max Farrington, immaculate as ever, wore a dark suit, white shirt and a blue striped tie. He waited patiently while Penny found the account he had requested to see.

Suddenly, leaning back in his chair, he quietly said, "Before we start, Penny, don't you think it would be better if I turned these account sheets?"

Completely taken aback, she just about managed to say, "If you want to."

"Of course I want to – I'm not exactly incapable." And he sounded rather annoyed. "Why in heaven's name you took it upon yourself in the first place is beyond me."

"Well, I thought you wanted me to," she replied, and she felt he was deliberately making a big issue of the whole thing.

He ignored that and, seeming to lose his patience, said, "The trouble is, you're far too bossy."

"I'm not bossy."

Now, she felt hurt.

"With an indulgent smile that just about touched the corners of his well-defined lips, he said, "I'm afraid you are, Penny Hathaway." Then, with a businesslike "Let's get on", nothing more was said.

At lunchtime, with only Nigel in the office, Penny couldn't resist asking, "Nigel, do you think I'm bossy?"

"Why?" Nigel wanted to know.

"Oh, just something that was said, that's all." And she tried to make it sound as though it didn't really matter.

"Well," he paused, and then, smiling, added, "well, you used to be, and then for a time you weren't, and now you're getting there again."

"Well, I don't think I am" was Penny's rather defensive reply.

"Don't worry – you do it in such a nice way, no one ever seems to mind."

But Nigel was right. For a while after Ben died, nothing seemed to matter, and now it was an uncomfortable feeling to know that, just as it used to, everything mattered.

Surrounded by pretty hamlets, Asher's only shop was on the corner of the High Street, and without any competition they sold everything from groceries and haberdashery to stamps and walking sticks. From March until November, in the small café at the back of the shop they served delicious fresh cream teas. Through the large picture window that gave full rein to the stunning views, it was possible to see the thought-provoking togetherness of the earth and sky. The winter months brought their own special beauty, and as the frost and snow clung lovingly to the pine trees Asher became known as the Little Switzerland.

The oval cricket ground was in the centre of the village, and as Penny drove through the gates the black-and-white pavilion was directly ahead. With all the attributes of a large and expensive summer house, its white veranda and picket fencing ran all along the front of the building. Standing almost in conjunction, and blending in perfectly, was the modern clubhouse.

Inside, the walls were painted in a delicate primrose emulsion, and the check curtains and matching tablecloths all gave it the feel of a homely friendly tea room.

Meeting her at the doorway, an extraordinarily tall lady with a lovely smile said, "I'm Maisie Pepadine. It's Penny, isn't it?"

Penny said it was, and then, before she could say any more, she noticed that Maisie's height had almost dwarfed a small lady who stood behind her. When she stepped to one side Penny could see she had short blue-rinsed hair and a cheerful round face.

Holding out her hand, she said, "I'm Gwen Shropshire. I'm so pleased you're going to help, Penny."

They were complete opposites, and she knew she was going to like them both.

During a little chat, they told Penny all about the club, and since both their sons played for Asher they were interested to hear all about James. When they asked how long she had been on her own, Penny said, "Nearly eighteen months."

She could hardly believe it was true.

Before starting on the teas, they were anxious to know whether she would be helping at all the home games, and Penny said she hoped to be able to. After pencilling her in on the rota, Maisie said everything was served from the long table at the top of the room. The routine was very much the same as at Langdale. Tea was usually after the first innings, and later they watched the cricket.

When Penny gave them the cakes she had baked, they seemed at a loss to know what to say.

Maisie found her voice first, and without pausing to take a breath she said, "Oh, Penny, you shouldn't have, but to tell you the truth we were hoping that you would." And then, turning to look at Gwen for confirmation, she said, "Isn't that right, Gwen?"

Thereupon Gwen obediently nodded her head in agreement.

At the end of the first innings there was a hectic thirty-minute tea break, and then, as the players began to go outside, things started to quieten down and one or two spectators appeared.

While she was busy clearing the tables, she suddenly heard Maisie say, "Max, are you going to try some of Mrs Hathaway's cake?"

Thinking it couldn't be possible, she turned around and heard the unmistakable voice of Max Farrington. Wearing sand-coloured heavy twill trousers and a black high-necked sweater, he was just about the last person on earth she had expected to see.

Completely thrown by the situation, she used his Christian name for the first time: "Max, whatever are you doing here?"

Now, Max Farrington had heard many women speak his name (maybe too many); but with the hint of a lisp and her slight drawl, no one had ever spoken it quite like that.

Giving her a searching look, he said, "I'll be back in a minute."

Coming to her with his tea and cake, he took a bite and thoughtfully gave it his attention.

"Maisie was right: it's very nice, Penny."

Murmuring, "Thank you," she still hadn't got over her surprise at seeing him.

With his next words, she felt at a complete disadvantage: "I believe James is joining us in June?"

While it was obvious he was a man who would be careful to keep his work and his private life separate, the fact he had never mentioned anything when she had been in his office yesterday made her feel even more uncomfortable.

Suddenly aware she hadn't answered his question, she abruptly said, "Yes, the second week."

Sounding genuinely interested, he said, I'm looking forward to seeing him in action. I believe his bowling's quite something."

On hearing this, all Penny's motherly pride took over. Forgetting her inhibitions and feeling an empathy towards him she wouldn't have believed possible, she told him about the difficult season James had last year.

When she finished, he quietly said, "Well, let's hope he enjoys being at Asher."

Then, not able to resist asking, she said, "How did you know James was coming here?"

Without hesitating, he volunteered the information: "I'm on the selection committee, and I go along to the net practice."

"I suppose you knew I was coming, then?"

"Yes."

He didn't appear to have any inclination to elaborate further, and after that there was an awkward silence. At a loss to know what to say, she was beginning to find the conversation hard work.

Then, surprising her, he suddenly said, "I'll look out for James when he comes along."

Feeling he would have a bit of support, it never occurred to Penny it might be just a polite remark.

Showing her enthusiasm, she blurted out, "Oh, Max, will you?"

Immediately she wished she hadn't, because as soon as she said his name his icy-cold stare made her feel as though a cloud had suddenly covered the sun.

Then, with a conversation-stopping "Of course", he excused himself and went outside.

This left Penny thinking what a rude and unpredictable man he could be. In her eyes he had the unforgivable trait of one minute being kind and friendly, only to follow it with a sudden hurtful indifference. Well, since she didn't intend to ask for his help ever again, it would be the last time he treated her in that way.

But she had enjoyed her day, and although seeing Max Farrington had made her feel unsettled, she thought if she kept out of his way things would be fine.

Things were beginning to change at Farrington's, and since this was almost unheard of the staff were none too pleased. The problem was, Max Farrington now required all the departments to supply a lot more detailed information, and, as everybody was quick to point out, this was going to be a lot more time-consuming.

Frank said it was time he retired and left it to someone younger, and since Tristan was the next in line he diplomatically said nothing. Sam said at his age he couldn't cope with change, and Tony said he didn't think the paint shop's system could be improved. While

Brian, who had never got to grips with any system other than his own, was going around with such a troubled face, everyone wanted to know if things were all right between him and Dot.

On most days, one manager or another went into Max's office, and Nigel would always sit in on these meetings. At the end of the afternoon if Max disappeared, everyone wanted to know how things had gone; and although Nigel said he couldn't possibly say anything, he always said just enough to make everybody fume.

The accounts office would be taking the brunt of most of the changes – Dot and Molly would now have to wait for Nigel's go-ahead before making payments. This meant that if there was a considerable delay in paying, there would be a constant stream of phone calls from irate suppliers. To put it mildly, Dot and Molly were none too pleased.

Farrington's had always had the reputation of paying their accounts promptly, but in today's climate Nigel said they were *too* prompt. He said nowadays it was all a game. Since everybody delayed paying their bills, Farrington's had to start using the same tactics.

When Dot and Molly had gone to see Max, he said although they might not like the changes, they had to be implemented. Greg grumbled that he would be spending most of his time chasing the departments for their late invoices, and Colin tried to placate them all.

Nick and Simon would be taking it in turns to go away on a four-day course, and Nick said Angela didn't want him to go; but since Nigel said (later in the year) the same was going to apply to Dot, Molly and Penny, they were so concerned about how it was going to affect them that no one was listening to Nick.

But it was Penny who was going to have the most unpleasant task. Now she would be putting pressure on those customers who paid on account each month; and since they were already struggling, the changes would only make things more difficult. Although most made their payments on time, Max wanted the monthly figure raised; and if they objected, their credit with the company would be stopped.

This incensed Penny, but when she went to see Nigel he said

there was nothing he could do – and anyway, he agreed with Max. Since Nigel was the one who told everybody what was happening, he was the one they all went to with their complaints; and if they got no joy, they went to see Max.

When she walked into Max Farrington's office, it was the first time (apart from saying good morning) Penny had spoken to him since she had seen him at Asher. If she thought it might have changed things, it hadn't. He still sat at his desk looking as remote as ever.

"Sit down, Penny." His voice was almost severe. "Now, I gather from Nigel you're not too happy about the new arrangements?"

"No, I'm not," she almost snapped.

Sounding irritable, he said, "Well, I have no intention of justifying myself. Nigel has explained my reasons, and they seem fair to me."

"Well, they would do, wouldn't they?" was Penny's rather sarcastic comment.

"What's that supposed to mean?" He was gritting his teeth.

"Oh, nothing." Penny shrugged her shoulders.

"Come on, Penny – you can do better than that."

So that was exactly what she did. With a passion he thought a few changes hardly justified, she let rip. Listening to her let off steam, he thought there was no sitting on the fence with Penny – she either approved or disapproved, and she didn't mind saying so.

When she had finished, he quietly said, "Right, so now we know where we stand, but it seems to me you've taken up the fight for the underdog, and you're wrong. This is a business I'm running, and things have got to change. My father may have chosen to ignore it, but we have to move with the times; otherwise" – and he gave her a piercing look – "we will all be without jobs."

He was no doubt right, but in true Penny fashion she had to let him know how she felt.

With a resigned look she got up to go, and as she did so he said, "Will you send out letters to those customers who will be affected by the changes?"

"Yes." And then, as she got to the door, she suddenly remembered she needed him to sign a cheque. Forgetting all about the animosity of the last half an hour, she pleasantly said, "Will you sign this cheque, please, Max? It needs to go today."

With a hand that was not its normal steady self, he took the cheque from her and wrote his signature.

Handing it back to her, he said, "Have you always found it necessary to challenge new decisions?"

"Only when they don't seem to be quite fair" was her rather perky answer.

Sounding exasperated, he said, "In other words, when they don't comply with Penny's rules."

"No, when they're just not fair."

But his "I see" actually meant he didn't see at all.

Max Farrington was not used to having his decisions questioned, and he was certainly not used to having to justify them. As she closed the door he was reminded of how, before Ben's illness, his father liked to say about Penny, "She's a good feisty Farrington's girl."

Today, for the first time, Max knew what he had meant.

"Damned good at her job too," he would add.

That was true, and after all that had happened he had been surprised to see her energy and interest in people had returned. She had argued their cause with such vitality it had made him ask a few questions about himself. He tried, but as usual when it came to his feelings he didn't get very far. Once it had been very different, but where, he asked himself, had it got him? Now he lived his life outside his emotions, and it had been a long time since he had felt anything other than the superficial needs of the moment.

But after seeing Penny so enthusiastic and spontaneous, he somehow knew she would face her emotions truthfully and without fear. So maybe, if he was honest, he would see that 'certain something' he always felt was missing from his life was probably his inability to become emotionally involved with someone again.

And then, with a cynicism that had taken years of dedication to achieve, he thought since he had never met anyone remotely like she had been, it was too late to try and change.

Culley Moor was the last little village before the bleak ten-mile drive to the rambling city of Hillside. So it was surprising (and, to a stranger, often inconvenient) to find the village had no shop, garage or local pub. In fact it had no amenities at all. These were to be found in the small town of Embridge, five miles before you came to Culley Moor, and there was nothing in Embridge to indicate it was the last place until Hillside to provide any services.

Then, a couple of years ago, a large hotel consortium had spotted the commercial potential of Culley Moor, and a few months ago a new hotel and restaurant had been opened, providing excellent food and accommodation. Yesterdays was now the place to be seen. With its 1930s art deco and quite alarming prices, Yesterdays (to the satisfaction of the locals) was fast becoming the venue of choice for the exclusive country-club set.

So when Julie rang and said "Everybody's talking about Yesterdays – shall we go?" Penny readily agreed.

They had booked a table some weeks ago, and they were going to go that Saturday evening. Since Julie lived in the direction of Culley Moor, Penny said she would pick her up.

Penny's instructions were to wear something 'posh', but she hadn't got anything she considered to be particularly posh, so she had bought a figure-hugging pale-rose fine woollen dress with a tight-fitting bodice and a gently curved neckline. Its softly flowing skirt ended just below her knees, showing to perfection her long slender legs. She also wore a pair of fashionable brightly coloured beaded sandals, and now that her hair was longer she looked about eighteen.

She rang the doorbell and Julie soon appeared. Penny thought she looked absolutely gorgeous, having skilfully managed (for Julie) to get the plain stylish look of 'posh' just about right. Penny's only reservation was the suitability of her deeply plunging neckline. However, since her dress was unadorned, her hair simply styled and her high-heeled black sandals perfectly plain, it seemed on this occasion, apart from the outrageous size of her gold hooped earrings, she had left it to the dizzying depth of her neckline to say it all.

To Penny (with her rather idealistic views) it said something that made her feel slightly uncomfortable; and although she felt disloyal, she hoped it didn't say the same about her. If Julie's clothes reflected her confident and flamboyant nature, Penny smiled when she thought what her little woollen dress said about her. Then, telling herself that things like that shouldn't matter any more, she forgot her silliness and looked forward to Yesterdays.

Like scorching-hot flames, the floodlights blazed into the red-brick building. With its iron-railed balconies and imposing canopied entrance Yesterdays looked like a scene from some extravagant film set.

Once inside, they were welcomed by a young man in evening dress, and with their booking confirmed they followed him into a large luxurious sitting room with pastel-green walls and a deeply piled green carpet.

After they had ordered drinks, he handed them a menu and Julie and Penny (along with half a dozen other people) were left to enjoy their surroundings.

They found themselves looking at palm trees, marble pillars and life-size statues. The name of each statue and other relevant information was engraved on a brass plaque below each sculpture. With well-defined lines reminiscent of the period, the ornaments were all painted in bright, bold abstract patterns, but compared to today's more elaborate styles the furniture (although comfortable) looked plain and almost severe. Yesterdays had an authentic 1930s feel, and the relaxing atmosphere and the apparent ease in which everything happened (presumably achieved by hours of practice) induced a feeling of pampered indulgence. It was quite a revelation to think some people were able to take all this for granted.

The menu was a comprehensive list of traditional and continental foods. After much deliberation, Julie chose the fish for her main course, and Penny chose the lamb. Then, catching up on the gossip, it didn't seem long before the waiter appeared.

"If you would like to come this way, ladies, your table is ready."

With the decor very much the same as the sitting room, one of the most attractive features of Yesterdays was the small friendly dining room. The fact it was so surprisingly small was not an accident. In their effort to faithfully recreate the past, they had remembered the importance of 'cosy and intimate'.

From where they sat at the top of the room, they had a good view of the other diners, and as Penny looked around she became conscious of someone trying to catch her attention. Then to her complete amazement she saw it was none other than Charles Farrington.

Smiling, she waved back, and as she did so she noticed Daphne by his side. Max was also there, and seated next to Max Farrington was someone about his own age. With her perfectly coiffed dark hair, and wearing a smart silver jacket, she was the personification of sheer understated elegance.

When Penny said, "Don't look now, but the Farringtons are only a few tables away," that didn't stop Julie. After a quick glance, her interest was instantly aroused.

"Gosh, that Max is something else!"

Having heard it all before, Penny gave a groan. "Julie, no."

With the arrival of the first course (there were six), the subject turned to food, and after working their way through all the courses, including choosing from the mouth-watering sweet trolley and sampling the cheese and biscuits, they ended their gastronomic experience with coffee and liqueurs.

During the meal, Penny tried not to let Max Farrington spoil things, but he had an ability to disturb her peace of mind, and she resented the fact his cool and aloof manner could make her feel edgy and uncomfortable.

Then, suddenly, she heard Julie say, "Watch out – Charles Farrington's on his way over."

With considerable care, he weaved himself around the tables. Then, putting his arm protectively on Penny's shoulder, he said how pleased he was to see her. After Penny introduced Julie (who immediately became all feminine charm), Charles asked if they would like to join his table.

When Penny hesitated (and Julie's eyes willed her to say yes) Charles said, "Come and have a little chat with Daphne. She'll love that."

Max must have guessed what was going to happen, because by the time they reached the table two extra chairs had miraculously appeared.

With Julie happily chatting away (the elegant person with Max was called Fiona), Penny turned to speak to Daphne. As she did so she noticed the feathery wisps of hair framing her face were now snow white. Wearing a lilac dress with a high collar and long sleeves, she looked every inch the family matriarch, but tonight there was a frailty about her Penny hadn't seen before.

Taking Penny's hand and holding it tightly, she said, "Max doesn't say a lot about the staff, but I was pleased to hear about Dot's engagement and Nick's wedding." So this was where Penny started to relax, and from time to time Daphne would say, "Now, tell me again – do I know them?" And she always did.

After a while Daphne began to talk about the past, and she fairly glowed when she remembered things Penny hadn't thought about for years, but Penny did begin to feel embarrassed when she realized how much she must have told Charles about Ben and the children.

But all this nostalgia was bringing back a life that was becoming increasingly unreal. Penny didn't understand why she didn't feel the intense pain she had been so accustomed to.

After Daphne said she was hoping to come with Charles to see James play at Asher, she asked about Lara, and Penny told her she was looking forward to working in the hospital.

Then Daphne suddenly said she would have loved to have a daughter, and then, looking fondly at Max, added, "As well as, not instead of!"

Giving her an indulgent smile, he looked amused. "I should think so too!"

With a quick look in Julie's direction, Penny could see she was in fine form. She leaned towards Max, touched his arm, ruffled his hair and laughed as she held his gaze. Since her dress appeared to be having the desired effect, all the stories she had heard about him seemed to be true. But Penny had seen all this before – it was not difficult to see how Julie's love life became so complicated. But she thought this time Julie might just have met her match.

As for Max, it annoyed him to see Penny gently holding his mother's hand, and, for some reason, when she occasionally gave it a reassuring little squeeze it annoyed him even more.

After a while, Charles said, "Come on, Daphne – let's all share Penny."

Before chatting to the others, Penny had a brief conversation with Fiona. After Fiona said she was only there for the weekend, Penny was sure she heard her refer to Daphne as 'Auntie'. Looking for a resemblance, Penny noticed that Fiona was as dark as Daphne used to be, and she had the same fine bone structure. Penny was hoping to solve the mystery, but she was confident of one thing: since Fiona didn't seem bothered by Max and Julie, it was highly unlikely they were a couple.

With a lull in the conversations, Max turned his attention to Penny: "So what do you think of Yesterdays?"

Not prepared to fall into the same trap she had fallen into at Asher, her rather short "I like it" gave him no chance to comment further. Then, thinking she had sounded rather rude, she tried to make amends: "Max?"

This was her natural way of saying his name, and she would have been horrified to think he thought differently, but to Max it always sounded like a long inviting drawl.

It was enough for him to answer sharply, "Yes?"

"Well, I was just wondering—"

Before she got any further, he interrupted, and this time his voice was gentle: "What were you wondering, Penny?"

But since she thought he was humouring her, she quickly changed her mind.

"Oh, nothing."

When he didn't pursue it any further, it only confirmed her suspicion that he found her boring.

The rest of the evening passed quickly. Fiona (she taught geography, but didn't say where) spent most of her holidays in one exotic location or another; and since she had some interesting and amusing tales to tell, they were the last in the dining room. By now Penny could see Daphne was tiring, so, looking at Julie, she said perhaps they should be thinking about leaving.

On the way home, Julie never stopped talking about Max; and when Julie said he had asked where she worked, Penny said, "He might ring you."

But Julie didn't think so: "He won't. I've met his sort before – you work for him, and he's not the type to play so close to home."

Penny smiled. "Sorry."

Julie just laughed. "Well, I can always live in hope."

Penny felt joining the psychology class had been the best and most helpful thing she had done. Marcus, with his dry sense of humour, logical explanations and the gift of gently putting life into perspective, had probably exerted the most influence.

Now the course was completed, she was really going to miss it.

Although not a day went by when she didn't think about Ben, she had finally accepted there was nothing she could do to alter the past. But remembering last year, and with James and Lara home tomorrow, she decided what she could do was to try and make this summer a happy one.

Whereas James was sensitive and rather stubborn, Lara (who now had her first serious boyfriend) was confident and assertive.

Lara and Adam had been together since the beginning of the year, and Penny generally spent her time reminding Lara not to neglect her studies. Since Adam only lived about ten miles away, they had seen each other in the Easter holidays, and on a number of occasions Lara had brought him home. Penny immediately liked him, but she could see it was an attraction of opposites. He was about the same height as Lara and just as fair; but whereas she was outgoing and bubbly, Adam was rather shy and almost diffident. Lara admitted he had a steadying influence on her.

Talk about music to her ears! The relief to Penny was like a harmonious symphony!

A few days before the end of term they were discussing the holidays when, for some reason, Lara began to talk about James. When Adam said his friend Jonathan played cricket for Asher they were both amazed.

Over the months James kept in touch with Jacob West, and one weekend he arranged to go to that Tuesday's cricket practice. With the prospect of being with Adam and watching Jonathan and James play, Lara was so excited she could talk of nothing else. When James came home after his net practice with his news, Penny thought the summer was going to be all about Asher.

James had been introduced to the players and to Bill, Peter and Max, and later he was thrilled to hear he was to be included in Saturday's game. When for the umpteenth time she heard the words "Max said . . .", Penny could tell Max had made a favourable impression.

When she asked, "Is he friendly?" James replied, "Well, he doesn't shout like Bill and Peter. He speaks to people on a one-to-one basis."

This came as no surprise. In fact it was just how she imagined him to be.

That Saturday, the second team were playing away from home, and Lara and Adam were hoping to go; Penny was down to help Maisie and Gwen.

In the brilliant sunshine, Penny could see the green hills fading into the distance. As the church's tall spire looked on in watchful silence, she thought Asher's cricket ground was one of the prettiest she had ever seen. But when she saw the long wooden benches she knew, from past experience, that unless you brought your own padded cushion they were only meant for the most dedicated of spectators. Most spectators made their own seating arrangements, and there was an assortment of deckchairs, garden chairs and stools. One old gentleman (so Penny was told) sat in a comfortable armchair his son brought along in the back of a large white van. Some people were reading books or newspapers. A few sun worshippers (with eyes closed) lay on the grass, and a few older ladies sat under sun umbrellas knitting. Waiting to cause mayhem, small children held their bats and balls at the ready.

The captains (about to flip a coin to see which team went out first to bat) were walking on to the pitch, and the players (in their whites) sat outside the pavilion and waited for the game to begin.

Maisie and Gwen decided that, with so many people outside,

extra sandwiches needed to be cut, another bag of crisps and tin of biscuits opened, and, with plates of small cakes, Penny's sponges could be carefully sliced and placed in the centre of the table.

At the end of the first innings, the tea break was taken. It didn't help that all the players expected to be served at the same time. Whenever anyone considered an umpire's decision had been unfair, the air was blue, and they spent the next half an hour apologizing to the tea ladies for their choice language.

Afterwards they prepared, for the spectators, fresh pots of tea, and cold drinks were made; and at the end of the afternoon there was just sufficient food for everyone.

Later, with everything tidied away, they settled down to watch the game, and almost immediately (sitting at the far end of the ground) Penny saw Charles and Daphne. At first she thought it might be better to stay with Maisie and Gwen, but when Charles spotted her, and she remembered how welcome he had made her and Julie feel at Yesterdays, she changed her mind. After a quick word with Maisie she went across to them.

Although she protested, Charles went to his car and came back with another deckchair, and Daphne said when they had seen so many people going into the pavilion she was pleased she had brought a picnic.

When Daphne reached for her hand, Penny noticed her fingernails were beautifully manicured, but where once there had been sun-kissed freckles there were now telltale brown age spots. Rather than dwell on the inevitability of getting older, Penny thought how entertaining and interesting Charles and Daphne could be, which made her wonder how the son of two such warm and likeable people could appear so cold and unfeeling.

After a while, Charles leaned over and insisted Daphne put on the sweater he was holding (it was quite cool, and he had always been very protective). Meekly doing as he requested, she then turned to Penny and asked if she had seen Max. When she said she hadn't, Daphne looked quite vague.

"I think he's with Gloria."

Just as Penny was thinking, 'Oh dear – not another one!' Max strolled towards them with Gloria. Somewhere in her late thirties, she was small, blonde and pretty.

Penny rather spitefully recalled the dry comment of Barrington Clarke: "They may look different, but I've seen those types before."

Max just about acknowledged her, but he didn't introduce Gloria.

When Daphne innocently said, "Penny's been helping with the teas," Gloria gave her a look that clearly said she didn't fraternize with ladies who served teas.

With Gloria chatting to Charles, Penny suddenly felt Max looking intently towards her. It was a baffling look – for one brief second those dark empty eyes had shown a spark of something she couldn't quite fathom, and then just as suddenly it was gone.

After the hot day it was now really chilly; and as earlier the heat had been stifling, Penny was only wearing a light summer top (which by her standards certainly wasn't discreet).

She was about to excuse herself and find her cardigan, when she heard Max say, "You need to put a jacket on."

And when she brightly said, "I'm fine," it obviously didn't please him.

"Well, you don't look fine to me," he replied, and his face glowered at her stubbornness. "For heaven's sake!" And he looked exasperated.

"Really, I'm fine."

And with this (although she couldn't believe how childish and silly she was being) she lightly brushed her lips against Daphne's smooth, delicate cheek and, smiling, said her goodbyes. Then she went back to sit with Maisie and Gwen.

With his four wickets for eleven runs on Saturday, James was hoping before the end of the season he would have a chance to play in the first team. Penny secretly thought he was good enough (after all, he had played in Langdale's first team), but since this was the aim of all the second-team players it was up to James to play consistently well.

He said very little about his job in the bookshop, and whenever

Penny asked if he was enjoying it he'd say, "Fine, Mum – it's fine."

But his cricket was quite a different matter. For the last two weeks his only conversation had been about Asher, Max and Peter.

Tonight he began another story of Max's cricket triumphs by saying, "You've probably heard this, Mum." Afterwards, when she said she hadn't, he sighed. "Mum, you must have! How long have you worked for Farrington's?"

Years ago, when Charles had known Ben was a keen cricketer (and a fast bowler, the same as Max), he would occasionally say, "Tell this to Ben – he'll like it," and then he would proceed to tell her some humorous tale involving Max. But all that was a long time ago.

When James went upstairs, Lara said, "Max didn't tell him any of that. It was Bill and Peter."

Penny had never met Bill and Peter, but they seemed to know an awful lot about Max.

When Lara told her James thought Max was a lot like their father, this really did upset her.

"I'll have a word with him – he's nothing like your father."

"Don't, Mum. If he knows I've been talking to you, he'll stop telling me things."

Lara said Max did sound a bit like her father, but she quickly added, "In a lot of ways he isn't, but James says he's patient and really listens. And guess what, Mum? He likes jazz." (Ben had been a keen jazz fan.)

James had also told her that after the previous week's cricket practice they went into the Ranton, and after talking to Max for a while he'd found him good company, and he'd said Max liked so many things their mother liked.

He'd told Max, "I can't believe how much you have in common with Mum."

Lara told her mother this.

Now, this was too much for Penny. She did not dare to think what James might repeat. She knew she must quietly find a way to stop him talking about her to Max.

It was Lara who put it all into perspective: "Mum, don't say anything. If it's helping him, that's all that matters."

Remembering last summer, Penny realised Lara was right. If she was honest with herself, she had wanted Max to take an interest. If James sometimes said things he shouldn't, well, it was hardly going to be of any importance to someone like Max Farrington.

One day, Dot's hair was in a bun of almost epic proportions. After months of seeing it loosely around her face, Nigel stepped back in horror.

"Bloody hell, Dot! It's enough to frighten the life out of Brian."

"Well, it doesn't."

After this sharp reply, she began to busily sort out the pile of paperwork on her desk.

After Beth had brought the tea and coffee round, Dot suddenly said she had been looking at houses with Brian, and their mums were selling their properties, and they all planned to live together.

She added rather shyly, "We're getting married at Christmas."

Simon's "Phew, Dot, there's no half measures with you. Fancy living with your mother-in-law!" didn't bother Dot.

In fact she said her mother had told her, "Now I can die happy."

To this Greg sourly commented, "Typical mothers!"

Molly couldn't contain herself. She was more interested in the wedding.

"Shall you wear white, Dot?"

Appearing almost embarrassed, she said, "Brian wants me to."

By now Molly was really into her stride: "Are we invited?"

Dot laughed. "Well, if it's left to Brian, all Farrington's will be invited."

With this, Molly went into one of her reveries.

"I think Christmas weddings are really romantic. Shall you have velvet?"

Dot said she hadn't thought about it – but Molly had.

"Winter clothes suit me best."

Nick, who had problems with his computer, was under his desk surrounded by wires. Since he would be away on a course next week, Angela wasn't very happy and he was under pressure.

Nick didn't operate well under pressure, but as usual he couldn't resist a dig at Molly: "Hold on, Molly – it's not your wedding." In her own inimitable way, she chose to ignore Nick.

Dot and Molly sat together, and Penny's desk was at the other end of the office. Carrying on a conversation wasn't easy, and sometimes she felt left out of things. If Nigel came in to have a chat, that was fine; otherwise he said their talking distracted him, and he became irritable. With a bit of ingenuity, Dot and Molly found a way around it.

If Nigel was particularly crotchety, and they had some gossip to pass on, one of them would come to Penny's desk and whisper, "Come down to the loo."

After a long phone call with an anxious customer (Max's new rules hadn't gone down well), Penny needed his advice. Knocking on the door, she went into his office, where, with his head down, he was writing. She noticed the amazingly deep-blue cuffs on his shirt, and she could see some of the streaks in his hair were almost white.

Looking up, he watched her walk towards him. She was wearing a cream button-through dress and her blonde hair seemed longer than usual, he thought. Regardless of all that had happened, she still retained an innocence he found deeply disturbing.

At first she stood by his desk, but after briefly telling him the problem he said, "Draw up a chair, and let's see what we can sort out."

With her chair beside his, there was no hint of any sweet-smelling aftershave; only the clean air of his masculinity filled the room.

He went through the accounts carefully, and after about twenty minutes, and a bit of compromising, the monthly payments were temporarily reduced.

With a quick thank you as she went to pick up the folder he'd earlier thrown to one side, his hand accidentally brushed against hers. Although his touch was as light and gentle as a butterfly's wings, for one fleeting moment her wayward emotions betrayed her, and she inwardly trembled. She was taken completely by surprise. It didn't make sense. For most of the time she found him difficult and remote, and for his part he usually treated her like an adolescent child. So how could this sometimes strange and aloof man have such an effect on her?

James was off to his cricket practice, and after promising to have a game of Scrabble with Lara, Penny remembered Chastie Hope's words: "It's all about time."

At first without Ben (although he used to tease her and say she invented words) she had thought she would never want to play Scrabble again. Then, knowing when James and Lara played they missed their father, she made herself join in. From this shaky start she had slowly found her interest returning.

Similarly, the house no longer felt so empty and strange, and she couldn't believe she had once contemplated living somewhere else.

When she and Ben first looked around, it had been neglected and run down. It needed a lot of hard work, but the price was still really beyond them. But, as a draughtsman with a local engineering firm, Ben had a good salary, and so they found the deposit, took on a sizeable mortgage, and never regretted it. Built in 1880 and named after its original owner, Meacon Holland stood at the end of a Victorian terrace with a small gravelled area at the front. The garden at the back had apple and pear trees, a long wide lawn and deep colourful borders. It had been Ben's pride and joy.

From the hallway, with its impressive mosaic floor, there was a front and middle sitting room, a dining room and an extended kitchen. Upstairs were four double bedrooms and a bathroom. It was a substantial home.

Over the years, with the help of family and friends, Ben had done a lot of alterations, and around the large kitchen table Penny had frequently seated more than a dozen people.

With most of the walls painted in a delicate cream colour, it showed to advantage the many pictures Ben hung on the walls.

In the sitting room was a small grand piano (inherited from Ben's maiden aunt), and, when she chose to, Lara played it well. It stood in a corner by the bay window, and, since she never put her music away, the top of the piano (when she came home) was generally piled high with music books. James's guitar and music cluttered another corner, and on the back wall (crammed to capacity) was a tall oak bookcase. This left just sufficient room for two small sofas and a table.

The middle sitting room was smaller, with a television set, two armchairs and a long settee. The walls were covered with Ben's pictures (landscapes with views of the sea had been his favourite), and even now it was very much his room. James and Lara still referred to it as 'Dad's room'.

Nowadays the dining room was hardly ever used, and sometimes Penny felt she could live in the kitchen. With the pictures Ben and the children had painted hanging on the walls, she was more content here than in any other room in the house.

Breaking into her thoughts, Lara appeared, and in a long-suffering voice she said, "What on earth are you doing, Mum?"

Saying she would have a quick shower before James came home, Penny went upstairs. Ten minutes later, in her short white fluffy dressing gown, she went into the kitchen and, after switching on the kettle, renewed the nail varnish on her toenails. Hearing James's voice, she called and asked if he wanted a coffee.

In a well-modulated voice, and sounding remarkably polite, he called back, "Two, please, Mum."

With wet hair and toenails, after making four cups of coffee (and never giving a thought to why James requested two cups), Penny walked barefoot into the sitting room, and nearly dropped the tray she was carrying. On the sofa, as if he had always sat there, was Max.

Before she could speak, he held up both his hands, and said, "I'm sorry about this, but I'm afraid James insisted I pick up a book he'd like me to read."

Thankfully, Lara was not in the least put out.

"Before you say anything, Mum, James has introduced us." Then, pausing: "I've persuaded Max to have a game of Scrabble."

Lara was so friendly you would have thought she had known him for years, but Penny thought she might have put him in an awkward position.

"Perhaps Max doesn't want to stay, Lara."

But he just smiled and said, "I don't think I can get out of this one."

While Penny was thinking of something to say, Lara didn't have the same trouble.

"I was going to play with Mum, but sometimes she cheats. Last week she added two letters and made 'WHAREPUNI'."

Before she got any further, James interrupted: "It was just a lucky guess."

Completely lost for words, Penny said the first thing that came into her head: "Well, I think I'll go and put something on."

James looked absolutely amazed.

"What do you mean, Mum? It's hot and you've already got on more than most people."

It didn't help matters when Lara piped up, "Take no notice – it's Mum's age."

Watching Penny, Max's thoughts ran riot. with no doubt little underneath her dressing gown, she didn't look old enough to be the mother of these two confident adults. Although he could see she liked them teasing her, for some reason he found himself feeling surprisingly protective towards her.

They all decided to play, and soon James and Lara (just as they had done with their father) were laughing and joking with Max, who (like their father) seemed to revel in their banter.

He sat opposite Penny, and she was so aware of him that when his eyes suddenly caught hers she felt he was the only person in the room.

Bringing her back to reality, she heard Lara saying, "Ignore anything Mum says, Max."

Looking amused, he light-heartedly said, "Is that right, Penny?"

Because of how she was feeling, she thought she sensed an underlying tension to his words.

Trying to answer as casually as she could, she said, "Of course it isn't right!"

Finally it was Lara who won.

When Penny asked Max if he would like a coffee, he said,

"Thanks, and then I really must be off."

Just as he was about to leave, Lara invited him for a return game, and when he hesitated Penny saw her chance to diplomatically avoid another such evening.

"Max is probably too busy, Lara."

But he quickly said, "No, no, that's fine. I'll look forward to it." And he really sounded as if he meant it.

Driving home, he didn't want to think why a simple game of Scrabble had been so enjoyable; but if he had, he would have realized that tonight was about much more than just a simple game of Scrabble.

For the last four weeks Max had been to Penny's house every Tuesday night, and for the last two Adam came over. After the first week (when Penny only made coffee) James said he had been starving, and couldn't she have done sandwiches or something? So that's what she did. A salad and the few cakes she baked went down well.

One night when she went into the kitchen Max followed her and asked if he could help. She was about to refuse, and then changed her mind. She thought, 'Well, if he wants to . . .'

With a rather abrupt "Do you know what to do?" she gave him the salad to prepare.

He smiled. "Of course I know what to do. I live on my own, remember?"

She replied with a rather sarcastic "Oh, I thought you had somebody to do everything for you."

His pointed "Not everything" had the desired effect, and Penny remained silent.

But she was becoming used to him, and she was finding he liked to be the one who set the tone of the conversation. If he wasn't, and if he didn't like the way it was going, he froze you out.

What did surprise her was how thoroughly he washed and prepared the salad. Determined to find fault, she decided he was far too fussy.

Over the last few weeks, she had grown confident enough to tease him, and although she knew he found it annoying (but it did help to disguise what she hoped was just her silliness) as she passed his chair she ruffled his hair. Seeing him put out of his stride didn't happen very often, but it gave Penny a certain amount of pleasure to know she was capable of producing at least some sort of response from him.

When James finally made the decision to play for Asher, Penny had told them at work; and after saying she would be helping with the teas, Simon had said, "Good for you! Langdale wasn't helping, Penny."

Then Nigel got it absolutely right when he said, "No use punishing yourselves with memories."

And that was exactly what had been happening.

So the first time she went to Asher she had seen Max, and (although she was careful how much she said) she told Dot and Molly, who asked if they could tell the others (and Penny said they could).

It wasn't long before she heard Simon shout across the office, "I hear there's no getting away from our Max."

Then everybody wanted to know how much she knew; but since she didn't know much, it spared her any further questions.

Every Monday they asked how Saturday's game had gone, but it wasn't often they asked if she had seen Max. Now, apart from anything else, she never felt she could tell them he'd been to Meacon Holland – she preferred not to have to say anything.

He was still distant at work. Whereas with Dot and the others he sometimes had a chat, he never did with Penny. But she didn't mind. This was better than having to acknowledge his kindness, patience and all his other attributes James was so fond of telling her about.

For an important one-day match at Tyler Park (about an hour's drive away) a first-team bowler was on holiday, and James had been given the chance to take his place. On the Sunday morning the weather was already hot (so far it was proving to be an exceptionally warm summer) and James left early to pick up two other players. Adam (who knew the ground) had given Penny the directions.

After a few heated words with Lara, and one or two wrong turnings, they were surprised to find Tyler Park so near to the motorway. After driving through a run-down industrial estate and passing rows of semi-detached houses, they found the entrance to the park at the bottom of a busy cul-de-sac. The huge iron gates were wide open, and they were so surprised to see the great expanse of green fields and woodland. It quite literally took their breath away.

Lara's "Crumbs, Mum, it's like finding a diamond in broken glass" made Penny smile.

Lara had arranged to meet Adam by the pavilion, so, following the map he had drawn, they passed a children's playground, a miniature railway, roundabouts and trampolines, and made their way along a densely tree-lined path. They soon left the noise behind. At times the heavy foliage nearly eclipsed the brilliant sunshine, but where it did peep through it brought another attractive dimension to the ever changing scene.

Penny was enjoying the walk, but Lara kept complaining.

"How much further is it, Mum?"

Then, just as she was about to say she didn't know, the path suddenly took a left turn and the pavilion came into view.

They met Adam by the pavilion. Although the grass on the cricket pitch looked smooth and well cared for, the same couldn't be said for the rest of the field. (Adam said the ground was also used for athletics and football.) With seating all around the pitch, most of the collapsible chairs were occupied, but they just managed to find three seats together, and almost immediately Lara began to unpack the picnic they had brought.

Asher were the first to bat. At two o'clock Tyler Park walked on to the field, and the opening batsmen followed. Although they needed to go for runs, it was a slow and uneventful start.

Batting at number nine, James didn't have the patience or temperament to be a batsman, but to be fair there were occasions when he managed to get a respectable number of runs.

James said Max was there with Peter, and it wasn't long before Lara spotted them.

Turning to Adam, she said, "Let's go over and have a word."

Since Lara hadn't met Peter, Penny thought it might be better to wait, but that was not Lara's style. Before she could say any more, she and Adam were gone.

When Asher started to chase the runs, they got careless and the wickets began to fall. Then just before tea they were all out for 194 (James put on eighteen). With so few runs on the board, any chance of winning was now down to the skill of the bowlers.

After queuing for cups of tea, Lara saw the thick chocolate gateau and pleaded, "Let's try some, Mum."

And so they did.

When the match resumed, Asher came on to the field, and Penny suddenly felt quite emotional.

Looking concerned, Lara said, "Are you OK, Mum?"

When she said she was just a bit apprehensive, Lara said she felt the same.

After nearly an hour, the opening bats were still piling on the runs. Asher had already made one bowling change, but it hadn't had the desired effect. At the end of the next over the captain threw the ball to James, and Penny hardly dared to look.

From the beginning they knocked him all over the ground, and James soon realized they knew precisely how to play him. Normally if he wasn't getting wickets, he was at least an economical bowler, but maybe he was too anxious to prove himself. His bowling was becoming extremely expensive. After a while the captain raised his index finger and indicated that this would be James's last over. Penny's heart sank.

This time James took an even longer run-up to the crease, but then, surprising the batsman, he bowled a slow, leisurely ball. There was a split-second's hesitation and, to the delight of the Asher supporters, the ball hit the batsman's stumps, and he was out.

With this boost to James's confidence, the last ball of the over was so fast it was unlikely the new batsman even saw it coming, and he was out for a duck. Having learnt his lesson, James was given more opportunities to bowl, and now he kept the runs down.

A change of bowling brought the loss of three more wickets, but the runs were still mounting up. Before the next wicket fell, the batsman (a real slogger) put on thirty-one.

Adam said even the tail-enders were pretty good, and with 163 on the board Tyler Park looked set to win.

Although James hadn't taken any more wickets, the captain seemed quite happy to continue allowing him to bowl. When his next wicket did come, he was lucky it didn't go for a six. Fortunately for James, the batsman failed to connect with the ball, and he had the pleasure of clean-bowling him.

Twenty minutes later, he dismissed an unsuspecting batsman for two runs, and then, in no time at all, he added a 'leg before wicket' to his credit.

By now Tyler Park were sensing defeat, and for a while things quietened down. Then James found himself facing the last man in. He hit the first ball for a four, but, after deciding to repeat the performance, he missed, and his wicket was lost. With the spectacular departure of Tyler Park, the Asher camp went mad.

Penny felt proud and for some reason tearful. After clapping James into the pavilion, she said to Lara that she was just going to walk to the end of the ground.

For all their ups and downs, Lara was very close to her mother, so, having a good idea how she must be feeling, she said, "I'm coming with you, Mum."

"No, you stay with Adam. I'll be fine."

With that, Penny slowly walked away from the crowd.

Once she was on her own the tears came. Thinking about all the 'if onlys' made her feel sad, but after seeing James so ecstatic she felt confused and guilty for feeling sad. But these days most things seemed to confuse her, and sometimes she felt she was living with a stranger.

Invading her thoughts, she heard a voice that was hauntingly familiar: "Penny, I've been speaking to Lara. Are you all right?"

It was Max.

Trying not to let him see she had been crying, she took a deep breath and spluttered, "Yes, thank you."

"Penny, turn round." His voice was so tender she felt she was drowning in a whirlpool of emotion, but nevertheless her back remained resolutely facing him. "Penny." And now there was an edge to his voice.

With her eyes red and swollen, she looked at him with such despair it was probably just as well she didn't know what he was thinking.

"If you come back to the pavilion, you'll hear something to please you."

"I can't. Everybody will see I've been crying." She still sounded tearful.

"Does it really matter? People will understand."

"How can they understand?" Now she sounded even more tearful.

"Come on, Penny – you know better than that."

Since he had no reason to be so kind, she could only think he must feel sorry for her, and she couldn't cope with that.

"I don't want people to feel sorry for me."

"There you go again!" And now his voice sounded harsh. "If anyone tries to help you, you're always so damned prickly."

With her hackles raised, she indignantly said, "I'm not." (But if she had been honest, she would have said, "Only with you.")

"Penny, you're going to miss it."

Although he was beginning to sound annoyed, she still made no attempt to move.

Then, with his patience deserting him, he softly said, "Do you want to miss seeing your son made man of the match?"

"Oh, Max, is he?"

Now all she could think about was James, and all Max could think about was the way she said his name.

When he gently put her soft, warm hand into his, it was such a perfect fit he felt on fire. As he looked at her tear-stained cheeks, something told him the 'no-commitment game' would never interest Penny. She was as determined and principled as she was caring and funny, and, he suspected, everything anyone could ever want. Then, telling himself he hoped one day she would find someone worthy of her, he rather callously let go of her hand.

Although she wished Max hadn't seen her so upset, he had been kind, and the reason why he suddenly (and quite carelessly) withdrew his hand was not something she was prepared to analyse.

James was talking to Adam, and Lara immediately asked, "OK, Mum?" And then as an afterthought: "Did you see Max?"

She said she was fine and she did see Max.

It seemed after the presentations everyone was meeting in the village pub. Before that, Lara was interested in the girl she had seen James talking to.

"Who was that I just saw you with?"

Looking embarrassed, James asked, "When?"

"About five minutes ago."

"Oh, that's Daisy."

"Who's Daisy?"

"Peter's daughter."

"Do you like her?" Lara was really pushing him now. "Why?"

Seeing he didn't want to answer, Penny came to his aid: "Lara, don't keep asking questions."

"Mum, he asks *me* things." Now she tried to look hurt, but not for long. "Are you going to take her out?"

"I might do."

"There you are, Mum – he does like her."

Suddenly James was more forthcoming: "Her mum died a few years ago."

"James, how sad!"

Before Penny had a chance to say any more, Asher's captain beckoned his players to join Tyler Park. (They were outside the pavilion waiting for the presentations to begin.)

Flanked by the players, Eddie Braithwaite was a large, thickset man. He (so it was said) had an equally large personality, and as chairman of the Sunday cricket league he began by saying how much he had enjoyed the match.

Then, as his enthusiasm spilled over, Lara nudged Penny: "Have we been watching the same game?"

But Penny found his enthusiasm appealing, and he was actually quite funny.

Eventually (and not before he gave a loud cough) he said there had been one or two contenders for the 'man of the match' award, but it had been decided to give the award to "the young player whose bowling nearly brought him to the brink of disaster, and then, confounding everybody, he went on to take six crucial wickets". After a comprehensive reminder of each lost wicket, Eddie paused, and taking a deep breath he announced, "Therefore the man of the match is James Hathaway."

While Lara and Adam jumped up and down, and the crowd clapped and cheered, James looked surprised and nervous. Then when he smiled it brought a lump to Penny's throat. After accepting the trophy and thanking Eddie Braithwaite, he said it was a moment he would never forget.

At this, Lara tearfully turned to Penny: "Mum, wouldn't Dad have been proud?"

Hugging Lara and saying he would, Penny was reminded of how acutely her children still missed their father, and she felt ashamed of her self-indulgent tears.

Now all she wanted to do was to please them; and so when Lara asked, "Mum, you don't mind calling in at the pub, do you?" Penny didn't mind at all.

After renewing her lipstick, Penny went to join the others, and Lara thought how attractive she looked. And then for the first time she wondered if her mother would always be on her own.

Penny saw Max right away, and, watching him laughing and joking, he didn't look at all remote and severe. She thought how he'd won over everyone in the office, where Sam said he was popular with all the staff.

James came to her.

"Mum, this is Daisy."

Penny smiled and said James had spoken about her, and then, noticing the look on James's face, she realized she had said the wrong thing.

Daisy was pale and fair; and although Lara said she was eighteen, Penny thought she looked younger.

All of a sudden, James seemed anxious for her to meet Peter:

"Mum, come and meet Daisy's dad."

Peter was quite tall, with a deeply lined friendly face. His dark curly hair was beginning to recede.

When two chairs became empty, Lara said, "Mum, you and Peter sit down."

When they discovered Peter's wife and Ben had both suffered from the same illness, they had plenty to talk about. He was undemanding and easy-going, and the fact he went on a bit didn't really matter. He talked about anything and everything, and Penny idly wondered why he had never married again, but when she went into one of her little reveries she could tell he hadn't even noticed.

Just when she was thinking it was about time they left, Max came over; since the crowd was thinning out, he pulled up a chair and joined them. He was quite talkative, but, after Peter's straightforward easy-flowing conversation, when he spoke directly to her that slight reservation in his manner was even more noticeable.

"So how does it feel to have your son made man of the match?"

Seeing his eyes twinkle, she thought he was teasing her, and then, thinking about James, she said, "After last summer, I can't tell you how it feels."

"Can't you, Penny?" And she found his voice unbelievably seductive.

Then, trying to explain herself, she said, "Well, I've changed. Everything's changed, and sometimes I don't seem to know who I am any more. Does that sound odd?"

"Not at all. When so much happens it does change you."

He said this with such certainty that she wondered what had happened to make him seem so sure, but, whatever it was, she felt she would never tire of listening to him.

One morning Max arrived early at Farrington's and as he sat behind the large oak desk that had once been his father's and grandfather's before him he looked every inch the imposing professional that he was. He had proved to be a popular boss. He had a reputation for fairness, and an empathy that Sam said "you've either got or you haven't." Well, for most of the time that was true, but if Max was not pleased he took no prisoners, and he would withdraw and become cold and distant. Now, reflecting on what he considered to be his old life, he had to admit it had been well ordered and very much to his own liking. But from a distance it no longer held any appeal. In fact it seemed rather shallow, self-indulgent and empty, and he was beginning to realize how much he was changing. The fleeting gratification of the no-strings-attached worldly glamour no longer held any interest, and he was amazed that it ever had.

Glancing out of the window, he could see Penny walking briskly across the car park, only to be overtaken by Sam. Her smile and her open enjoyment of whatever Sam's tale was that morning made him remind himself that commitment had never been on his agenda, but he found it disturbing how often his thoughts strayed to Penny. So he deliberately went back to his desk and made a couple of phone calls regarding the work being done on his cottage at Krayton.

Max's cottage stood on the edge of the village. It was pretty and charming, and looked almost untouched by time. Whether or not Max quite saw it like that was anyone's guess. With a colourful front garden and a manageable garden at the back, it had two lawns, and apple and damson trees.

Inside there was a comfortable sitting room and a somewhat smaller dining room, and Max was having the kitchen extended to include a shower and toilet.

Upstairs had five bedrooms – three on one side of the long but rather narrow corridor, and two on the other side. A family bathroom faced you at the far end of the corridor. It was quite impressive. With the help of Sam's decorating skills, Max was hoping to move in by Christmas, but always with Sam's note of caution: 'weather permitting'!

Although Penny was the first to arrive in the office that morning, she was quickly followed by Simon, and she knew he couldn't wait to tell her about his Saturday night. Now, if things hadn't gone well for Simon, he did tend to bend Penny's ear. Having got used to his tales, Penny had a fairly good idea when things had gone wrong! She knew things usually started with great promise and then rapidly went downhill, but Simon's disappointments were becoming more and more frequent.

So in a long-suffering voice Penny asked, "So what went wrong this time, Simon?"

"Well, I met this really attractive girl at the beginning of the night, and when I said I'd give her a lift home she said, 'Fine.' When I got outside her house I couldn't believe what happened next!"

Now Penny rather anxiously said, "Simon, I don't think I want to know!"

"Oh, I'm not going to give you all the details. Just let's say she was pretty frightening!"

Since this was such a change for Simon, curiosity got the better of Penny: "Why?"

Simon thought for a while, then, obviously trying to find the right words, said, "Well, just let's say she was bloody forward."

"Oh, Simon, why don't you try looking in other places?"

But Simon sounded quite frustrated and rather sharply asked, "So, Penny, where do I find these other places?"

Now Penny had to think, because to be honest she had absolutely no idea. So she quickly said the first thing that came into her head: "Well, how about a walking club, or even a night class?"

Then suddenly Max appeared. She had seen his office door was partially open, and she had assumed that Max had not yet arrived. But when he turned to Simon and jokingly said, "Bad night, then, Simon?" Penny realised he must have heard most of the conversation.

Simon was not in the least put out. He quickly went through the evening again, adding, "Penny thinks I go to all the wrong places, don't you, Penny? But where should I go?"

Max, with a glint in his eye, looked at Penny and asked, "Well, where should he go to, Penny?"

Now, since she had no idea, and she was beginning to feel embarrassed, she rather shortly said, "I'm sure you know better than I do, Max!"

He didn't reply. He just smiled, turned around and went back into his office, only this time he carefully closed the door.

When Dot asked Penny if she was staying in at lunchtime, and Penny said yes, Dot seemed pleased.

"Good – we can have a little chat."

As Dot walked back to her desk, Penny wondered why slowly, over the last few weeks, Dot's distinctive bun, which she usually wore high on the top of her head, had descended from its dizzy height. It now rested comfortably in a stylish chignon in the nape of her neck. This was not the only thing that had changed. The latest skirt Dot had worn had been noticeably shorter, and for the first time ever there was a glimpse of her leg between her ankle and the hem of her skirt.

This had raised the unlikely comment from Nick of "Glory be!"

Just as Penny was sorting out her lunch, Brian came into the office. Before he had become engaged to Dot, if he was going into the town he would open the office door and call, "Hi. Anyone want anything?" And that would be it. But now he went straight to Dot's desk, and after a little chat (Nick said he came in for his orders) he would cheerfully ask, "Anyone want anything?"

For those who knew Dot and Brian, there was definitely a subtle change. At first when Dot became engaged her way of dressing took a sudden and rather dramatic change. Some days she would wear her hair loosely around her face, and her skirts, although still long, lost some of their exuberance, but all this didn't last for long. Soon Dot's bun returned in all its former glory and her skirts were only a little less flowing than they used to be.

Penny was having her evening meal with James and Lara when suddenly James said, "Mum, you know there's only one more match at Asher."

Having seen the tea rota, Penny said she knew. In truth she hadn't wanted to think too much about it. She had loved having them both at home, and even welcomed the general air of chaos they created. Penny had to admit it hadn't always been like this. But now she appreciated most things in a way she had never done before, and she was beginning to dread the quiet voice of silence. While she felt that living alone was something she would never come to terms with, she would never have admitted it to others. James and Lara were both saying they hoped she wasn't going to find it too difficult being on her own again. James did say he hoped Penny would go to Asher's usual end-of-season buffet and dance at the Ranton; he did, however, point out that he would be back at university. After Penny had reassured them with "I'll be fine," Lara said, "You should be going out with someone. You know what Dad said."

And Penny remembered.

Lara was now saying, "Peter likes you, and just imagine you and Peter, and James and Daisy."

And actually Penny could.

Warming to her subject, Lara said, "And what about Clive at church? Didn't he and Dad go to a couple of England cricket matches?" Penny nodded that they had, so Lara continued: "And you and Dad were really supportive when his wife died."

Clive had been (and still was) very kind and thoughtful, saying, "Whenever you're ready, Penny, we can go out for a meal sometime."

But James was saying, "What about Max? He always seems friendly."

In seconds Lara was saying, "Oh no, Mum wouldn't suit Max at all."

"Why not?" James asked.

"Well," – Lara thought for a moment – "I really like Max, but if he ever gets married, and somehow I don't think he will, he would choose someone in-your-face attractive and clever, but someone who would be quite happy to let Max, well, be just Max because, let's face it, it's too late now for him to change."

This made James want to come to Max's defence, because he thought that was not the Max he had got to know. He said, "Well, perhaps that's how Mum would be!"

Lara was quick: "Don't be silly, James. Mum's far too confrontational for someone like Max."

And then, with all the confidence of youth, James declared, "Well, he might just enjoy the challenge, and Mum can be very entertaining."

Then it was remarkable how quickly they lost interest. After helping with the dishes, they both went to their bedrooms.

Left alone, Penny thought about the coming months, and she decided she would try and keep things simple. Now, since Penny had long ago learnt that, for her, keeping herself busy was the best therapy on offer, she quickly went through her plans for the run-up to Christmas.

There was going to be Sunday lunch with Ivy and Beryl from church, then she would help with the Christmas fair at St Luke's, then the carol concert and supper, and then she would no doubt go out with Julie. All of these things were, to Penny, her little comfort blanket. Then of course there was Dot and Brian's wedding, which was going to be on the Saturday evening after everyone finished work on the Friday for Christmas.

At the beginning of March next year she was due to go with Nigel on a course (which everyone else had gone on earlier this year). Since they would just be staying for the Thursday night, Nigel said that weather permitting (and at the beginning of March it should be improving) the journey home on the Friday was doable, saving them having to stay on the Friday night.

Penny knew she was (as Julie put it) wishing her life away, but at the moment it was without doubt helping.

As Penny drove to Asher for the last home game of the season, onlookers would have seen someone with a pretty and kind face. She also had a faint air of vulnerability about her, which she seemed totally unaware of.

When she arrived at the cricket ground, there were already more people than usual, and from the moment she appeared she was kept busy. Then, with just a short respite before tea, Penny was able to have a little chat with Gwen and Maisie.

Maisie said that during the winter months, as a way of keeping in touch, they met on Wednesday evenings at the Ranton. They chatted and took part in the pub quiz while the younger members played pool or darts, and generally made their presence felt. Maisie said by the end of January they would already be making plans for April, and the start of the new season, and Penny couldn't think of a better way to get through the winter than to talk about April in January.

Listening to Maisie and Gwen, Penny realized there was a lot to do before the cricket season began in April. When Maisie asked if she would like to join them on Wednesday evenings, Penny quickly said yes.

The tea break was particularly busy, and the next hour was hectic. Then the next innings began, and things quickly quietened down. Most people were now sitting outside.

Later when she saw Max he was with someone who quietly signalled 'country class'. She was clearly enjoying the attention she was receiving, and Penny thought how well suited they appeared to be. Then, rather to their surprise, Max came over and introduced Mandy to Gwen, Maisie and herself, and, contrary to expectations, she was really warm and friendly.

From the beginning Penny enjoyed her Wednesday evenings at the Ranton. She usually sat with the same little group; but during these evenings she did notice that people tended to circulate, and she thought she would begin to do the same. If Peter was around he would sit beside Jenny, but tonight he was working away from home as a quantity surveyor. This did sometimes happen. At first Penny sat with Gwen and Maisie, and when Max appeared he came straight over to sit with them.

Turning to Penny, he said, "No Peter tonight, Penny?"

When she said he was working away, he made no comment. After a while, when there was only the two of them, Penny was starting to feel rather uncomfortable so she remained quiet. She thought, 'If he's not making any effort to chat, neither will I.'

Then, unable to cope with the growing tension, she rather indifferently said, "Is something the matter?"

And, holding her gaze, Max said, "Why? Should there be, Penny?"

Shrugging her shoulders, she flippantly said, "Not as far as I know." Then, having had enough, she quickly said, "I should be going."

"Why? You don't usually go so early."

Resisting the temptation to say, "How do you know?" she said, "Well, it's very hot and noisy."

"Could it be that you're missing your Peter?"

"No, and he's not *my* Peter" was Penny's sharp reply.

"Isn't he, Penny?" And now Max looked quite serious. Then, looking directly at him, she said, "Of course he isn't!"

"Good – that's fine, then."

Penny replied, "Max, what do you mean by 'that's fine'? If I asked if you are with someone you wouldn't tell me, would you?"

And he coldly said, "No."

But now when she saw him at the Ranton, she noticed he always kept his distance; and since she found that sometimes his company could inhibit her, she thought it was probably all for the best. But why should he inhibit her? Well, maybe it was because one morning, when Max had only been at Farrington's for a short while, he had asked Penny to bring him the week's banking figures, and as she had passed the statements to him their hands had briefly touched, and Penny had been really taken aback by how aware of him she had been. From that moment she had never felt entirely at ease in his company.

In an effort to try and make a new life for herself, Penny had often accepted her friends' kind invitations to socialize. Some she had really enjoyed; others, well, perhaps not quite so much. But she thought this was the best way to find her way. However, she had encountered many hurdles, and made many mistakes. Now, to her horror, a Penny she didn't understand (and she sometimes felt quite shocked by her thoughts) was beginning to emerge.

When Julie had said they should meet more often, Penny agreed, and she decided she would go to the Ranton every other week. Julie's optimistic approach to life had always attracted Penny because, whatever her disappointments (and in her love life there had been many), she always managed to remain upbeat. Penny really wished that Julie could find the right one, but Julie liked the good-looking, still-in-love-with-himself type of man and then she wondered why these relationships never lasted. Over the years Julie had said many true things, but she never really learnt from her often sad experiences.

One occasion Penny particularly remembered was after Julie met Max for the first time at Yesterday's. Julie later said he seemed to be one of those people who find it hard to commit and are usually too fond of the chase. Not that Penny could ever see it happening, but since it was not in her nature to cope with that sort of emotional involvement she decided she must try and be as natural with Max as she was with everyone else.

One night Penny was going to the social evening at the Ranton. Although she was certainly more confident about what she wore, she still gave far too much 'air time' to whether her attire was suitable or not. On this occasion the new Penny was wearing a deceptively plain grey dress. Although it had a long narrow front opening, it revealed nothing. It was a cursory nod to a raunchiness not usually associated with Penny.

The inside of the Ranton was typical of a village pub. There were a number of rooms, all used for different occasions.

When Maisie and Gwen had first asked Penny if she would like to come to their Wednesday-evening get-togethers, they had also told her a lot about the pub and its traditions. At the end of a dimly lit corridor there was a large room for dancing, with a small stage for either a band or a DJ. The walls of the public rooms were covered in old sepia photographs, mostly of the village prior to the First World War, and alongside these were more-recent pictures of the village over the years. Gwen and Maisie had said it was a family-run business, owned by Doug and his wife, Fran. Josh, their son, was the chef, and the dining-room area was the domain of Rachael, their daughter. Harry and Percy, who were both retired, helped with any odd jobs when needed. Now, the only problem here was that Harry and Percy always found the most difficult way of doing anything, but they all got along together.

Doug would sigh and say, "Well, if it keeps a happy ship!"

When Peter saw Penny, he came across and said, "You look nice, Penny," and she thought there was nothing complicated about Peter.

They went to listen to the entertaining DJ for some time, and when they returned Max was talking to Maisie and her husband,

Bob. When Maisie complimented Penny on her dress, Penny thought that, from the disapproving look on his face, Max didn't agree. When Maisie and Bob excused themselves, Peter, who had just seen his old friend Reg, did the same.

Before leaving he turned to Penny and said, "Are you going to dance with Max?" And then he was gone.

Looking at Penny, Max asked, "Are you?"

With a slow waltz just beginning, Max held Penny's hand and they joined the other people on the crowded dance floor. The DJ was evidently playing his record on full volume, but Penny didn't mind because this song happened to be one of her favourites.

She quietly began to sing, "And I will always love you," and then found herself gazing at Max, who completely surprised her by almost whispering, "And I will always love you-oo."

Then for one minuscule second Max's eyes betrayed him, and he looked at Penny as though he had never seen her before. No one said a word, but now Max held her just a little closer (and, for all her good intentions, he might have been the only other person on the dance floor).

After a couple more dances, Max, in a rather shaky voice, said, "I think we should join the others, don't you?"

For the rest of the evening Penny felt comfortable and relaxed, and Max seemed to go out of his way to be chatty and entertaining. That was until Penny said she should be leaving, and Peter insisted on walking her to her car. With a decidedly frosty face, Max just about managed a curt "Bye."

Michael had been the vicar at Penny's church, St Luke's, for many years. He was well liked and popular. With a physique more suited to a disco bouncer than a Church of England clergyman, he had an unusually soft and melodic voice. That was until sometimes during one of his rather long sermons he thought he might be losing his congregation's full attention. His voice then became a commanding boom. But his parishioners took little notice – much to their amusement, they said Michael had a special voice for every occasion. Since he was diplomatically aware that his congregation could be quite sensitive to anything they thought might be contentious with regard to Church matters, so he usually approached any subject with a cautionary 'generally speaking', and would allay any doubts with the words "Now, you know I can only speak generally." And it worked every time.

With no children, Michael's wife was considerably older. Sally (or Sal, as he affectionately called her) was tall and rather masculine in appearance. No one quite knew what she had done before marrying Michael, but she certainly knew how to get the best out of people. Since Michael often went well beyond what could reasonably be expected of him, his parishioners were aware of the quality of his pastoral care. So when sometimes he got things wrong – and sometimes he got things spectacularly wrong – he would in his own inimitable way sort it out, and his parishioners tactfully left him to it.

Penny had arranged to meet Pam (her friend from church) outside the local retirement village. This was a long, low one-storey building. Each of the apartments had a large French window which overlooked a well-cared-for grass area. Inside, the atmosphere was friendly and warm, and each of the long corridors had a theme, displaying photographs of the 1940s, '50s and '60s stars of stage and screen and the football icons of the day. This evoked a nostalgia the residents enjoyed, and it created a comfortable sense of the past.

When Pam arrived with other members of St Luke's, they all went inside. Over the last few years Michael had taken their harvest-festival service, and a lot of his parishioners came to the village service. Chairs in the long hall had been arranged in rows facing the small stage at the far end of the room.

Penny and Pam had met Godfrey the previous year. Although he was in his late eighties, he still played the lovely grand piano which now stood in lonely isolation at the back of the hall. Godfrey was now sitting in front of an old treadle organ. With its darkish-yellow keys and grey worn stops it looked as though it hadn't had an easy life. When Zoe suddenly appeared, Penny asked her why Godfrey was not going to play the piano.

Zoe sniffed and said, "It's that old organ. You can't keep him away from the darn thing."

Now, Zoe had been one of the first residents to move into the village, and what she didn't know, quite frankly, was not worth knowing. She might have had the appearance of a frail and ancient old lady, but she was actually one of the sharpest, most interesting and most entertaining characters you could ever hope to meet.

Penny was sitting at the end of a row, so she could see Godfrey pedalling away as though his very life depended on it. When he began to play the introductory bars of the next hymn, Penny assumed it was going to be sung to a tune she was not familiar with. Then she quickly realized that Godfrey was playing another well-known hymn.

Turning to Zoe, Penny asked, "Does Godfrey know he's playing the wrong hymn?"

Zoe said in a voice that implied she had long lost patience with Godfrey, "Oh, leave him! He's getting really deaf and he's probably tired."

Afterwards Penny and Pam did wonder whether Michael might mention it, but he didn't.

Once a year the sales department held an open evening, and the organization and responsibility for this was in hands of Frank, the sales manager, and his staff. Mostly it was attended by local businessmen, and anyone who could afford the luxury of a new car every year. Mainly due to Frank's meticulous planning and the hard work of his staff, it was always a success. In addition, over the last few years Farrington's had put on an open evening which involved all the departments. These evenings usually attracted a much younger customer. At this time Dot and Brian tended to have almost daily disagreements, generally over some trivial matter. They soon blew over and affected no one, but Nick wondered if this year things might be different.

Simon wisely said, "Don't be fooled – they enjoy these little spats."

Faith was a new member of staff in the service department, and she had immediately caught Simon's attention. She was quite shy and demure, and was a spot-on reflection of her name.

Since Simon usually pursued the rather loud and in-it-for-a-good-time sort of girl, Dot voiced a note of caution. She said, "You don't mess around with girls like Faith, Simon."

And Molly couldn't help adding, "I should think you've done enough messing about, Simon."

And he couldn't have agreed more.

With the open evening fast approaching, staff were asked, where possible, to lift-share. This would then leave more space in the car park for visitors. Penny was picking up Molly, who lived only about two miles down the road, and Penny virtually passed her house every morning.

Max went about seeing that everything was going to run smoothly, but Tony from the paint shop said, "His father's behind all this. He couldn't come in without any help and organize an open evening."

Tony appeared disgruntled, but it was doubtful if that was the case. It was just, as Nigel liked to say, "Glass-half-empty Tony!"

What to wear for an open evening had always been discussed at great length, and Nigel had been known to call from his office, "Bloody hell, ladies – give me a break!" But recently Penny was finding that deciding what to wear, or what not to wear, was no longer a big issue. Although she liked to look her best, all that angst seemed to have disappeared.

That night Penny wore a green skirt and white polo-necked sweater. She and Molly were on the tea-and-coffee stall, and there was a real buzz in the showroom. This could have been due to the fact that Max had decided to give the event plenty of publicity. Having been kept constantly busy, when Max appeared and asked for a coffee Penny pleasantly obliged.

Roy (a mechanic who had worked at Farrington's for as long as Penny) winked as he passed, and said in a loud and cheerful voice, "See you later, Penny."

Max, who had been standing nearby, turned to look at Penny and rather sarcastically asked, "Will he?"

But Penny never answered.

Molly and Penny stayed on to help sort things out for the next morning. Walking across the now almost deserted car park, they were both tired and ready for home. Reaching her car, Penny opened doors and she and Molly thankfully got inside. After several efforts to start the engine, they realized it was, as Molly put it, as dead as a dodo. Molly said she would give Penny a lift to work in the morning, and they hurried back towards the showroom, where they could see the lights were still on.

At the door they walked straight into Max, who laughingly said, "You're going the wrong way, ladies."

Molly explained what had happened, and that they were going to ring for a taxi, but Max wouldn't hear of it.

"I'll drop you both off."

To Molly's "Oh, there's really no need" Max rather abruptly said, "It's more or less on my way, Molly."

Penny sat in the back of the car, and thought, 'When he's dropped off Molly, whatever shall I talk about?'

But she needn't have worried because, without turning to look at her, and in a voice that was decidedly distant, Max said, "I'll drop you off first, Penny."

Maybe because she was so surprised, she said nothing.

When they arrived at Penny's, she heard herself saying a polite thank you.

Molly, who suddenly seemed to have taken an interest in her surroundings, rather gushingly said, "I'll pick you up in the morning, Penny," and, with a rather formal goodnight from Max, Penny got out of the car.

She walked up her short and narrow garden path, and it wasn't until she was inside the house, and had put on the lights, that Max drove away.

On Sunday, Penny went for lunch with Beryl and Ivy. Since she always enjoyed their company, every few months, after church, they would go to the same little pub some miles away. Penny always drove because Beryl and Ivy didn't drive. They were both recently retired. Although they were physically completely different – Ivy tall and rather awkward, rarely operating outside her comfort zone, and Beryl more relaxed and easy-going – but their natures were completely in tune. Over the years they had found the best way for them was to eliminate anything that didn't fit into their cosy little world. They both worked on the theory that if you had no influence on a matter, it was no use wasting your time and energy on it. Since they were both valued members of the church, everyone accepted that it was just Beryl and Ivy being themselves. Each of them was an only child of older parents, and now they lived on their own. It was a close friendship born of equal needs. The other side to them was the quiet way in which they were always there when anyone needed any help. For them, a simple thank you was all they could cope with, and it was woe betide anyone who was too vocal in saying they had been the recipient of their kindness. That was when Beryl and Ivy would withdraw into themselves. One of the reasons for this was that they believed that small deeds done are better than any big promises.

One morning Greg and Colin said how hectic everything appeared to be, and, hearing this, Nick immediately turned to Simon and said, "If those two think it's hectic, it's bloody hectic."

That could have been because Greg and Colin rarely got involved in anything that could be described as office politics. They both kept their heads down, and for most of the time remained pretty invisible. They were utterly reliable and were considered to be a tremendous asset to Farrington's. Greg, the assistant accountant, was the perfect foil to Nigel, who liked nothing better than to say that he felt he was always working under pressure. Greg's patience and good nature were an invaluable help in keeping Nigel's erratic blood pressure under control. Colin had sole responsibility for the company payroll, combined with the title of office manager. Now, since the office virtually managed itself, Colin was able to attend to his payroll duties with phenomenal dedication.

Suddenly Max's office door was flung open, and Max stood with blood pouring from his wrist. It was dripping down the front of his shirt, and gushing upwards to his face. For one second everyone seemed to freeze, and then Penny quickly got up from her chair and went to get the first-aid kit.

Max was still very much in control, and he demanded to know, "Why Penny?"

"Because Penny is in charge of first aid," they all replied.

Nigel came out of his office and helped with the larger first-aid box. Then Penny's training came into practice, and she calmly went into the required procedure. With the help of a tourniquet, the blood flow gradually slowed down. Nigel said he would take Max to A & E, but he asked Penny to come with them. No one had any idea how it could have happened, and Max was saying nothing, but this didn't seem the time to ask. The bleeding was now nothing more than a trickle, so Max insisted there was no need for Penny to come with them, but Nigel said he couldn't cope with blood. He said he wasn't very good in this sort of situation, so he would prefer it if Penny came.

They went through the side door of Max's office, and down a flight of stairs which led into the back of the car park. At Nigel's request Max sat in the back of the car with Penny. Max made it perfectly clear that he didn't want Penny to come, but she took absolutely no notice. She took her first-aid duties seriously, and otherwise she continued to ignore him.

With Max's wrist starting to bleed heavily again, they went to the admissions desk and were told to wait – they would be called as soon as possible. When Max's name was called, he said he would go in on his own, but Nigel thought someone should go in with him.

He quickly said, "You go, Penny."

And to this Max just said, "Fine."

At this point, they both thought that the sight of so much of his own blood was quite naturally getting to him.

First the nurse took them into a small cubicle, and then within minutes they were taken into a much larger room, with a bed, a wash-hand basin and a large open cupboard containing all sorts of medical equipment. Sitting at a long, narrow desk was a lovely smiling nurse. With a confident and reassuring manner, she briskly and in a no-nonsense voice told Max to sit on the bed in an upright position. She promptly supplied him with two pillows.

By now a young doctor had appeared, and with a needle in

his hand he said he was going to give Max a couple of painkiller injections.

The nurse in a tone of voice you could tell she used frequently said, "Are you OK with needles?"

And Max, with a rather superior nod of his head, said, "Of course."

The nurse, who was not at all put out, went on to say, "All you men are the same," and then added, "You'd be surprised how many pass out and then end up on the floor."

Turning to Penny, she said, "Most men are not great with needles. I should hold his hand if I were you." And then, as an afterthought, she added, "I don't know how you men would manage without us women."

The Doctor smiled and agreed. He no doubt had heard it all before, but the general chit-chat helped to put patients at ease.

When Penny first held Max's hand, he resisted, then suddenly his grip tightened until Penny thought her hand would break. When the Doctor had finished he told Max to see his GP in about ten days to have the stitches removed.

Now, with Max at his most charming, he thanked the Doctor and nurse, but once in the corridor, with a cool "Thank you" Max abruptly let go of Penny's hand.

Although feeling pretty uncomfortable, Penny brightly said, "That's all right. I would have done the same for anyone."

And his dry retort, "I know you would," hung in the air.

As they walked back to Nigel, Max looked at Penny and said, "I shall have to recompense you for your outfit."

"You certainly will not!" was Penny's quick response, then adding a belated thank you.

Nigel seemed relieved to see them. Max looked more like one of the walking wounded than the alarming sight he had presented when they had first come into the hospital. Nigel said he would drop Penny off to change, and then after taking Max home he would return to take Penny back to work.

Max explained to Nigel what had happened. Years ago Charles's father had had a high wooden bookcase built in his office, and to this day no one had been particularly fond of it. It was cumbersome and very much of its time. Its awkward corners and sharp edges were a nightmare to negotiate. Max was not the only one to have injured himself on it, but no one had done so as badly as Max.

When Max strode into the office the next morning, the only reminder of yesterday was his firmly bandaged wrist. After thanking everyone for their concern, he said he was now feeling fine. Before going into his office, he asked Penny if she would bring him yesterday's banking figures. Sitting behind his desk in his dark-grey suit, he looked his usual immaculate self, and Penny thought how Molly always insisted it wasn't only his clothes that caught people's eye, but it was something in the way he wore them. He then took the banking sheets off Penny with just an absent-minded word of thanks.

Although the heating was turned off, it was still unusually hot in the office. Taking her jacket off, Penny revealed her flimsy white blouse and camisole top. Simon and Nick, who had already been told off by Molly for looking and acting so bored and fed up, immediately spotted the chance for (as they would put it) a bit of fun.

Simon called loudly across the office, "Hey, Penny, did you know you can see through your blouse?"

Penny turned to Simon and said, "No, you can't."

But in chorus Simon and Nick said, "Oh yes, you can!"

Dot shook her head and said, "They think they're at a pantomime. Take no notice of them – they haven't got enough to do."

But Penny just turned around and said, "Lucky you!"

While Max had been with Nigel, he had left Nigel's office door open, but now, with more than a slight show of irritation, Max loudly closed the door.

This provoked Dot to say, "Now look what you've done! They must have heard every word."

When eventually Max came out of Nigel's office, Molly said he had a really frosty look on his face.

Just before lunch, Sam came into the office, and you could tell he was anxious to pass on all his latest news. Sam could successfully turn his hand to most things, and everyone knew that for the past few months he had been helping with the work on Max's cottage. Now it seemed that, with the furniture chosen, Max was just waiting for the experts to fit his carpets and hang the curtains, and by all accounts he was hoping to move in next weekend. Sam was full of this news. He was in his element, from the details of Max's kitchen extension to the disasters of the plumbing or the non-appearance of some workman or other. His blow-by-blow description of the electrical rewiring was most amusing.

After Sam's departure, Nigel wearily said, "Well, now all we have to do is wait for the next instalment."

One other snippet of gossip from Sam was that Max was having, well, not exactly a housekeeper, but someone who was going to come in for a few hours each day. Sam had already met Janet, and he said how likeable she was, and that Max was very lucky.

With two older children who had families of their own, Janet lived in the village with her husband, Steve. Quite how Sam knew this was probably down to the fact that he was a real people's person.

With Christmas only a few weeks away, Christmas decorations were going to be put up in the office. They had been given a fifteen-minute extension to the lunchtime break, and Dot was always the mastermind deciding where each decoration should hang – which was usually in the same place as it had hung last year. Molly was second in command, and Penny just enjoyed helping. Nick had wondered, with Dot getting married in a few weeks' time, whether she would have the same enthusiasm as in previous years, but if anything she had more. As usual Nigel had gone out, but he always came back early so as not to miss out entirely.

Greg and Colin went for their lunch and arrived back at exactly the same time as most days.

Every year each department had its own real Christmas tree. Before Charles retired he had got himself a good deal with a local garden centre, and each year they continued to supply the company's Christmas trees. With its height and the spread of its branches, it was lucky that one of the Christmas trees fitted so well into the alcove at the back of the office. Every year Dot or Molly put the large silver star on the top of the tree, but this year Nick said it was Penny's turn. So she quickly went up the ladder and put this last decoration on the tree.

In the spirit of Christmas, you could count on Simon to make at least one cheeky comment. This year's "I've got a cracking view down here, Penny" rather backfired when Nigel's "Like the office, Max?" saved Simon from any terse comment from Max.

Penny's exasperated "Simon!" really put a dampener on the whole proceedings.

Penny had been trying to balance a set of figures the bank had requested first thing in the morning, and since she had not envisaged any problem it was late in the afternoon before she started to look at them. When Max asked how things were going, she had to admit not very well. So he suggested that Penny brought the accounts into his office and they could look at them together. An hour later, with the general office deserted (and because she didn't want to appear ungrateful), she was still sitting with Max, who was insisting they went over the figures yet again. Since Penny had already diligently gone through them twice, she was fast losing patience.

She felt that, far from helping, Max was being very controlling and had virtually taken over. It seemed that whatever he said he expected her to agree with him. Penny felt they were going at a snail's pace and getting nowhere. She thought Max was just not listening.

She suddenly got up from her chair and said, "You don't need me, Max – you just don't listen." And then unfortunately she couldn't stop. "But then you never do. And if you do listen, you just say, 'I don't think so, Penny' or 'Maybe'." Now Penny was almost shouting. If she had noticed Max's face she might have stopped, but she hadn't.

He stood up and, unable to suppress his anger, looked at Penny and said, "Don't you ever dare speak to me in that way again."

Then defiantly she said, "I just have, and if I want to I shall again!"

At this point Max seemed to lose his well-guarded self-control.

He unceremoniously pulled Penny towards him and furiously and relentlessly kissed her. And then, taken completely by surprise by her response, he gently began to take her into his own special world. His kisses became softly persuasive until getting to know each other became overwhelming.

Then, without warning, Penny reluctantly moved away, only to hear Max's hoarse almost trancelike "Penny, for God's sake!"

And she knew she had just done the almost unforgivable.

Before Max could say any more, Penny's impassioned "I'm so sorry – I just can't" hung in the air like words in a solitary Sunday-morning confessional.

She knew that Max would see that it never happened again.

Then quickly Penny put on her coat, and, without a backward glance, she left. On the way home she thought about the first time Julie had met Max. She liked him, and she said the Max's of this world can be kind and charming, but what you don't do is get involved with them. Prophetic words! Tonight Penny knew she had come so close to doing just that.

On the last working day before Christmas (that year it was on a Friday) the general office always held their buffet lunch. Beth enjoyed getting together with the other junior members of staff, who were responsible for their departments' food. Colin and Greg joined in, but this year Dot was at home, seeing to all the last-minute preparations for her wedding. Simon and Nick, the double act, therefore had no Dot to keep them in check. Molly did try, but she was not as effective as Dot. They were funny, and it was an enjoyable couple of hours. Before they all left, Max came in and wished everyone a happy Christmas. He hadn't joined in.

As Nigel said, "Who wants the boss around at these times?"

Max said he would try and call in tomorrow night, and Nigel said, "Since most of Farrington's staff are expected, Max isn't going to be able to let his hair down."

Penny was going to church with Molly, and most of the other female staff were hoping to see Dot and Brian get married. Brian's younger brother was the best man, and Dot's friend Vera was her maid of honour. The little church Dot attended had a plaque inside saying the church was built in 1856, and it was so small there had been some concern as to whether there would be sufficient seating. Brian stood at the chancel steps looking slightly nervous; when the organ began to play he visibly relaxed. Dot came down the aisle on the arm of a family friend. Wearing a pale-pink suit with her hair in its now familiar chignon, she looked a happy demure version of the Dot everyone knew.

Penny danced most of the evening with Nigel, and by nine thirty no one had seen Max.

Then suddenly Nigel said, "Max has just appeared."

However, they remained on the dance floor and it was some time before they sat down and Max joined them.

If Penny had wondered how he would be, she needn't have wondered, because he was exactly the same self-assured Max that she was used too.

When Nigel excused himself, saying he must have a word with Dot and Brian, he turned to Max and said, "She's all yours now, Max." And with that he went to find Dot.

For a minute they both looked at each other in silence, and then Penny said, "Max, whatever we say, it won't be what we really want to say."

His "Probably" wasn't very convincing, but then he continued with "What I don't think you understand, Penny, is that when I want to be with someone the feelings have to be mutual. I don't need to be with anyone who doesn't want to be with me."

And Penny thought, 'That's put me in my place.'

Thankfully, before she could answer (and maybe it was as well that she hadn't) Nigel reappeared.

Turning to Max, he said, "You'll have to excuse us, Max. I'm just about to put Penny through her paces again."

With a dismissive "Sure!" Max got up from his chair to allow Penny to follow Nigel on to the dance floor.

As he did so, he gave her a look that seemed to pierce her very soul, and Penny thought, 'Whatever it is between us, it's not over yet.'

Within the next half an hour people were becoming increasingly concerned about the weather. The snow that had been lightly falling for most of the evening was now heavy and drifting, and the cars in the car park were becoming completely obscured. Since most people didn't want to spoil Dot and Brian's evening, they had probably stayed on longer than they would normally have done, but now, at eleven thirty, apart from a few seasoned diehards most people were starting to leave. Penny couldn't help feeling relieved that James and Lara were at home that night. The plan had been that tomorrow they would meet Adam and Daisy for a day together, but at the moment that seemed as though it was highly unlikely to happen.

Just after seeing Dot and Brian leave (with a lot of help), Penny, with Molly and Albert, went to find Penny's car. She had parked it at the top of the car park, which at the time seemed like a good idea, but now they realised it was going to be impossible to drive home, so along with the vast majority of people they went back to the hall and joined the long queue waiting to phone for a taxi. The hall was to remain open until everyone had left.

Suddenly, with a look of astonishment, Molly said, "Look — that's Max's car."

There it was parked right by the exit, and Max was walking towards them. No one dreamt of asking him how he'd managed to find such a convenient parking spot.

Instead Molly said, "We've come with Penny, but there's no way we are going to be able to get to her car, so we were going to ring for a taxi."

Before Penny could say anything, Max immediately said, "I'll drop you off." Then, with Molly and Penny about to protest, he smiled and pointed out that he'd done it before.

The journey to Molly and Albert's was a nightmare, and it was a relief when their house came into view. Molly said if they wanted to they could stay the night. After thanking them, Max said he'd just push on. It would most likely be a slow journey, but he felt sure he'd be able to drop Penny at home and then drive on to Krayton. Penny thought that shouldn't be a problem; the problem was (as so often happens) that the heavy snowfall had taken everyone by surprise.

Just after leaving Molly and Albert, Max suggested that Penny should ring James and Lara (Penny had told him they were at home tonight), and this was when Max's car phone came into its own. Penny told them that when they were nearer to home she would ring.

The snow got heavier, and it swirled ominously around the car. Penny was getting increasingly concerned.

Unable to help herself, she said, "Max, I think something dreadful could happen, and nobody would know."

Now, since the traffic was bumper-to-bumper in front of them, and the same behind, Max drily said, "I think it's highly unlikely, Penny."

She tried again, but this time she said, "Max, we don't know how long we are going to be here, do we?"

He said they didn't.

With that she said, "Well, in that case, Max, you can't just sit there and say nothing. It's making me feel uneasy."

Max replied with a brisk "Right, what would you like me to talk about?"

Penny said, "Don't patronize me."

But they did chat, and Penny found herself telling him things about herself that in different circumstances she might not have done – just general little things about her life. She was surprised how easily he responded and did the same, and Penny began to wonder whether in many ways she had misjudged him; or were there many different facets to Max's character? She suspected the latter.

So perhaps (and she smiled at the thought) she should say, "Will the real Max Farrington please stand up!"

When they eventually arrived at Penny's, Max realized that it would be foolish for him to try and drive to Krayton. James brought Penny's wellies, and a pair of his own for Max. They didn't fit perfectly, but they helped.

Once inside, Lara took charge, and Penny could tell that she and James were enjoying the drama.

Lara then said, "Put your dressing gown on, Mum. James has gone to find one for Max."

When Penny came downstairs, Max was already wearing his. Lara said she had made tea and put the fire on in the sitting room, and James had made up the sofa bed for Max.

"Now, just relax for five minutes and we'll see you in the morning."

Then Lara smiled and said, "Well, I guess it's nearly morning now!"

The situation was so surreal that there was lots to talk about. Penny, more as a conversation opener than anything else, started to go through the events of the evening, and she mentioned his remark "I don't think you understand, Penny, that when I'm with someone . . ."

Then she suddenly noticed his stony face and she stopped, but not before hearing him say, "Well, rest assured it won't happen again."

And she quietly said, "I know."

After that she diplomatically prepared to leave, but before she did she said she wanted to see if it was still snowing. It was, and Penny thought from the safety of inside how magical it looked.

In her enthusiasm she said, "Oh, Max, you must come and have a look."

And then, standing behind her, he did, but it is only fair to say that perhaps Max didn't find it quite as exciting as she did.

Penny closed the curtains and, not realizing Max was so close, she turned around and was almost in his arms.

As she looked up he bent his head and with a sharp intake of breath whispered, "Penny."

And then his lips were gently brushing hers, but this time she stayed and this time she met Max's needs with needs of her own.

For a while Penny didn't recognize herself or recognize Max's strained "You wouldn't let anyone else – you wouldn't, Penny."

This time Max was careful not to ask too much.

Next morning everyone surfaced late. Penny decided to cook a substantial breakfast. She then began to wonder what to expect when Max appeared. When he did, just for a moment he looked at Penny with eyes that were achingly tender, and then she heard his bright good morning and she knew normality had returned.

It seemed before they knew it the light was fading. Although James and Lara hadn't been able to go out for the day, they had seemed to enjoy talking to Max. After a few phone calls, the snowplough came through and Max's neighbour said the road into the village was now passable; so in the late afternoon, after thanking everyone, Max left.

James and Lara said how much they had enjoyed talking to him, and Penny had noticed during the last year how good he was with young people. Since this had been his profession, she thought there must have been a good reason to bring him home to Farrington's. Maybe it was simply that Charles was due for retirement and Max was his only child.

Asher's New Year buffet and dance was always held in the local village hall.

When the tickets went on sale, Maisie said to Penny, "We are only a small club, so, if you'd like to, bring a friend along. After all, it's open to everyone."

So Penny asked Julie, who immediately thought it was quite exciting. As she pointed out, any social event was an opportunity for her to meet someone, and Penny knew without Julie she wouldn't want to go.

Christmas had been spent with Penny's older sister, Judi, and her husband, Tom. They were without any children of their own, and had always been close to Penny's family. Since their parents had died when Penny was very young, Judi had always seemed more like a mother figure, and over the last few years she and Tom had been her greatest support. Then, as they proudly watched Penny slowly build a new life, they wisely withdrew a little.

With James and Lara at their own parties, Penny was almost ready for when Julie arrived. She had long given up all the anxieties she used to have about what she should or shouldn't wear, and tonight, although she was pleased with the result, had been no exception. Aware that it was the village hall, and she didn't want to appear overdressed, she was wearing a straight red skirt and a fine grey cashmere sweater that had been a Christmas present from Judi and Tom. It clung seductively in all the right places, and with a long silver necklace and grey strappy sandals she felt comfortable.

When Julie breezed in, Penny thought she looked stunning. It was a mystery why she was still single. Wearing a short black dress that was stylish and understated, but with a deep plunging neckline that Penny found alarming, since it lacked even the slightest nod to convention, it was all credit to Julie that she wore it with such ease and she got away with it.

No one had said whether Max would be coming, and Penny secretly hoped that he wouldn't.

They deliberately hadn't gone early, but Penny hadn't expected to see so many people. Almost right away Peter came across to them with Carl and Kevin quickly following. Penny vaguely knew them. While Peter introduced everyone, he seemed particularly pleased to include Julie. Penny knew Julie was about to be the centre of attention and she was pleased. She didn't mind at all, because she had giggled with Julie, saying that the men would give her a lot of attention (which she loved), while the ladies . . . Well, that remained to be seen.

Sometime later Penny saw Max dancing with Maisie and then with Gwen. When she was dancing with Peter he was deep in conversation with Sandra, who occasionally worked behind the bar. Max seemed very sociable, and for some reason Penny didn't quite like it. It could be that at times like this she realized that Max was on his own by choice, because finding someone would never be a problem for Max.

When Max came over to their table, Julie became the focus of his conversation; when he asked her to dance, they remained together for the following three or so dances. The time was going quickly and, against her expectations, Penny found she was enjoying herself. About eleven thirty the DJ announced that from now until midnight he would be playing only slow ballads, and almost immediately the dance floor became crowded. Peter, who Penny thought was quite taken with Julie, had just asked Julie to dance, and this left Max and Penny alone at the table. This was the first time they had seen each other since Max had stayed at Penny's that snowy night after Dot and Brian's wedding.

At first there was the usual awkward silence, and then Max said, "Dance with me, Penny."

But Penny pointed out how crowded the dance floor had become.

Max gently led her on to the dance floor, saying, "We'll be fine." Then in a voice that sounded rather tight and husky he said, "I want to dance with you Penny!"

And Penny couldn't help thinking, 'Well, it's taken you long enough to ask me. I must be at the bottom of your list.' But of course she said no such thing.

Within seconds someone had bumped into Penny, pushing her further into Max's arms, and with a cheerful "Sorry!" the culprit was on his way. But as she began to move away, Max's hold tightened and he held her so close she could scarcely breathe.

That was how they stayed until Penny heard him say, "You smell nice." It was then that she became aware of Max in the same way she had done that night in his office and the snowy night he'd stayed at her home. When Max moved back her head, she found herself looking into eyes that were bright with an unfathomable emotion, and then she heard him say, "What are you doing to me?"

Now, very probably out of pique, or maybe even frustration, Penny said, "Are you sure you know who you're dancing with, Max?"

And suddenly he changed and cynically said, "Obviously not!"

When the dreaded midnight came it was nothing like the ordeal that Penny had anticipated. On the way home she was surprised that although Julie had been suitably flattered by Max, she only really wanted to talk about Peter. Penny wondered if Julie had recognized that Peter's interest in her combined with his sincere unassuming nature could be the start of something good.

With James and Lara about to go back to university, Penny was not looking forward to the suffocating silence that she found so unsettling. This winter, for the first time, St Luke's along with other churches in the diocese decided to support a charity calling itself Another Way. During the winter months Another Way supplied hot drinks, soups and sandwiches (and support if asked for) to the city's homeless, and, along with quite a few other people, Penny put her name forward as a volunteer. She went to a meeting where everyone was asked to give up one evening for the next four weeks. (Each church volunteered for one month.) Penny was surprised how much was involved in what appeared to be the simple task of distributing hot drinks. They were told that some people refused help altogether and others accepted quite begrudgingly. Some would chat; others would not. Each volunteer was given leaflets to distribute, explaining where help could be found. Another Way supported vulnerable people, and only they knew if their circumstances would allow them to accept help.

Penny's slot would be on Wednesday nights, so she rang Maisie to say she wouldn't be at the Ranton for a while. Volunteers worked in pairs, and her partner would be Reuben, who had just taken a rather late retirement. Reuben was a busy little man, small and slightly built. He still had wisps of sandy-coloured hair. With movements that were quick and jerky, his sole purpose in life was to please; and since he had spent a lifetime trying to perfect this art, it was quite remarkable how often he failed. The reason for this seemed to be that in trying so hard he often irritated and alienated people. This was gently pointed out to him, but it never deterred or dampened Reuben's enthusiasm. Penny found that his busy and industrious nature actually helped to make the Wednesday evenings seem more normal.

The charity workers operated in the back streets of the city, where everything was in a state of neglect, yet still standing in all the squalor was an old grey-stone church building. Although it had been vandalized and robbed of its dignity, its high spiral tower still stood intact and it seemed to keep a silent vigil over all it surveyed. Inscribed on the stone above the church's entrance, almost in open defiance of time, were the still clearly visible words 'The Place Where Hope Is Given'. No more than 100 years after the building was erected the streets that once led to the former proud and prominent church bore testimony to what can happen when all hope is gone.

Maggie and Pat were the only people to engage Penny in any sort of conversation. Their ages were a mystery (Maggie did appear to be the elder), and each line on their face told its own sorry story, yet they were both keen to say that no one but themselves was to blame for what had happened to them.

But Reuben (and Penny agreed) thought that, whatever the truth, they were not people who had squandered their chances; they were people who had never had chances to squander. For them, their only solace had been in the destructive use of drink and drugs.

Since returning to work in the New Year, Penny had felt that, although perhaps not particularly noticeable, Max's manner towards her was even more cold and remote than before.

One day when she was finding it difficult to access some information that Max had requested, she felt there was no excuse for his abrupt "Well, surely it can't be that difficult to find!" Maybe it was just as well that she didn't know this was something she might have to get used to.

One morning when Penny went to the bank, Shirley, one of the cashiers, gave her a large scroll-like package and asked if Max would sign the relevant paperwork. So that afternoon she went in to see Max and asked him to sign the paperwork as the bank had requested. Since he asked no questions, Penny assumed he must know what it was all about. As he began to write his name, the paper itself seemed to have other ideas. It seemed determined not to make it easy. Every time he began to sign his name the paper would roll up. Penny, who was sitting at the other side of his desk, watched in amusement.

Then she leaned forward and started to unroll the paper, and as she did so she cheerfully said, "I'll hold it, Max. That should make it easier."

For Max, the situation was fast becoming too much, and his frustration was compounded by the way she said his name.

He looked up and, with eyes that had suddenly darkened, he almost croaked, "Have dinner with me on Saturday, Penny."

And, completely taken by surprise, she said she would.

From then it became a regular Saturday-night pattern. Penny

123

knew for her own peace of mind she should stop seeing him, but for now she just couldn't. (Well, at least she told herself, 'Not yet.')

Although they mostly liked the same things, they did enjoy agreeing not to agree. Penny was aware that on the occasions she did question Max he didn't really like it at all. If they had both been honest, they would have known that it was the spark between them that made the mundane seem so endlessly attractive.

So now, though it was not exactly how Max would have liked, they did inevitably begin again where they had left off. However, this time they simply found their own special way forward. One day Penny made some remark about their Saturday evenings, and Max said, "Well, I think at the moment we're enjoying each other's company, don't you, Penny?"

And Penny knew then that she should have walked away.

Since Penny took understanding yourself to a new level, she was aware that many of her views would be considered by most people as slightly odd, old-fashioned or, quite frankly, boring. Since she had married when she was quite young, she had never done the boyfriend scene, so she was totally at a loss to know how to deal with Max's charismatic charm. What she did know was that, although he kept it well hidden, he was actually a kind and gentle man.

His 'at the moment' had made Penny realize why he supposedly had a long line of discarded relationships. She remembered how he had said, "When I want to be with someone the feelings have to be mutual." And while she perfectly understood, she wondered what happened when it was no longer mutual. She would like to think that maybe, just maybe, it would be different with her.

She could hear Julie saying, "That's what we all think, but it's that gentle charm that causes all the problems."

Most mornings Simon was one of the first to arrive, but one day he was the last. To put it mildly, he was a shadow of his usual upbeat self, and almost immediately he shared the reason. It appeared that last night Faith had finished things. Simon was devastated. He always looked extremely smart, but today it seemed he had just thrown on a jacket over the clothes he had been wearing last night, and the result was a surprisingly dishevelled Simon. When Colin sheepishly asked why, Simon said he had wanted Faith to know how differently he felt about her than he had about any of his previous girlfriends, and Faith quite naturally had demanded to know all about his previous girlfriends. Then, once she knew, she said she would never be able to trust him again.

Nigel, with all his years of experience, said, "Not a good move, I'm afraid, Simon. Some things are best left well alone."

Dot too was soon to give her considered opinion. This morning her clothes that no longer flowed with carefree abandonment – her blue skirt hung rather sedately and her top clung just a little to Dot. It has to be said that this style suited her. Her bun was firmly arranged high on the top of her head (which was always a bit of a giveaway sign as to how Dot was feeling), so today she probably intended to be efficiency personified. Having listened to Simon, she did try to be kind and sympathetic, although occasionally she couldn't resist a little dig.

She said, "I always told you, Simon [and she had], that one day it will happen to you, and that will be the only way you'll ever understand."

Penny hadn't contributed much to the conversation.

But Nick, it seems, got it about right when he said, "Hold on a minute, Simon – you're quite a lot older than Faith, and she's not been around like you. I'll bet it came as quite a shock."

And that really summed up how everyone felt.

At lunchtime, Penny had no reason to go into town, so Nigel, who was having one of his working lunches, called her in to have lunch with him. After a while Max appeared, and seeing Penny looking so comfortable with Nigel he suddenly felt unreasonably annoyed. Since he'd never had any experience of jealousy, he had no idea this might be why he felt so cross, but he walked into the office and sat down on the chair beside Penny. (Nigel always had two chairs on the other side of his desk for visitors.)

Now Max pleasantly said, "Can anyone join in?"

Then, since in any situation involving Penny he only saw Penny, he immediately noticed how elegantly she crossed her long slender legs and for some unknown reason he felt even more annoyed.

As Max had been out all morning, he hadn't heard about Simon, and after Nigel told him what had happened Max said he thought Faith seemed a nice girl, and he was sorry Simon had taken it so badly. He then rather flippantly added, "He'll soon get over it – it's happened to most of us at some time."

And Penny couldn't help wondering how many times it had happened to Max.

So far that year, Penny had only been to the Ranton on a couple of Wednesdays, but she was there for the cricket social evening, held on the last Wednesday before they started to make plans for the new season in April (they did this every year). When Penny arrived she went to sit with Gwen and Maisie, and it wasn't long before Peter joined them. Since the players were looking forward to the start of the season, there was a real party atmosphere. With James and Lara not home until the beginning of June, James, like last year, was going to miss the first few games.

When he knew Penny would be going to the social, he'd said, "Get all the info you can, Mum."

So Penny was looking forward to hearing what the plans were going to be for April.

When Max appeared he came to sit with them; and although he was amusing and he certainly seemed on form, he hardly acknowledged or spoke to Penny. Under different circumstances this wouldn't really have mattered, but when they were alone . . . well, that was something Penny just didn't want to think about. Even less did she want to think about how Max made her feel tonight. At least now she knew she had to face the unpalatable truth that there was only one thing about her that interested him; and since she was not prepared to be his convenient 'friend' she felt, if only for the sake of her pride, she had to stop seeing him.

Due to the heavy snow and the remote location of the venue, Penny and Nigel's accountancy course had been cancelled. Nigel seemed relieved, and so was Penny.

Although Simon was making every effort, he and Faith were still not together.

Nigel said, "Back off for a while, Simon, and see what happens."

After Wednesday night at the Ranton, Penny knew she had to tell Max that this Saturday would be the last time she would meet him, though she spent all week looking forward to seeing him on Saturday evenings. She knew something very important was missing between them, and she knew exactly what it was; but she doubted very much if Max did, and that was the problem. She also feared that Max's gentle persuasion would win in the end and, if the rumours were to be believed, once the chase was over it wouldn't be long before Max lost interest.

But of course it didn't feel like a chase at all. That was because Max could make you feel it was all about a very special you.

However, not everything had been on Max's terms – at least Penny thought she could walk away pretty much unscathed (but of course that was not entirely true). In fact she found it all very confusing because at times Max fleetingly showed some real and deep feelings, and then he would quickly retreat into himself. For most of the time he seemed hidebound by his own rigid self-control, and Penny had only once seen him break these 'rules' (and that was the time in his office). She had come to the reluctant humiliating conclusion that anyone could take her place.

She began to wonder what Max would say when she told him. He was not used to having to plead with someone to stay – after all, with his reputation, why should he?

As usual Max arrived at seven thirty. Although Penny was always excited to see him, tonight she had a lot to think about.

From its position at the top of the hill, the imposing white facade of the prestigious restaurant looked down on the prettiest chocolate-box cottages you could ever imagine. Inside reflected all the charm and character of the village, from the starched white tablecloths and the immaculately dressed waiters to the dark oak ceiling of the discreetly decorated dining room. It all helped to create the perfect relaxing night out.

Looking around the room, Penny could see that most of the

tables only seated two people. Having read the week's menu, she noticed that on Sundays they boasted a fine four-course roast dinner, and she thought, 'I'll bet these tables will be arranged to accommodate far more people than are here today.'

Suddenly, without any warning, there came a yearning that things might be different, but Penny's outgoing, everything-must-be-spoken-about nature was the complete antithesis of Max's inability to speak about how he felt.

Once Penny had hoped that she might be the one to hold the key to understanding this kind but intense and complex man. Then she had slowly (probably like many before her) come to the conclusion that whoever it was, it was certainly not going to be her. But what she did know was that this restaurant was a place where relationships began, not ended. And that was at the very heart of the problem, because what sort of relationship (if any) did she have with Max? Always at the back of her mind was the degrading feeling that she would be easily replaced.

Now, seeing Max sitting opposite her, Penny thought how much she was going to miss him. But one of the main reasons for her decision was Max's haunting words: 'at the moment'.

When the time came she struggled, and instead settled for a weak "Shall we leave things for a while, Max?" It was just about the last thing in the world that she really wanted to say.

Then, after an awkward silence, there came Max's rather strangled "Why?"

Penny had never thought for one moment that he would ask why, so she felt herself starting to flounder. How could she adequately explain to someone like Max, who she suspected looked on any show of emotion as a sign of weakness?

She found herself incoherently saying, "Max, I've always tried to understand you, and I've usually managed to convince myself that since we see each other every day at work, and you're my boss, that is the problem. But I have found that when we meet socially, and not on our own, you more or less ignore me. Most of the time I feel invisible, and that hurts, Max. Why do you do it?"

His rather indifferent "I just have to, Penny" made her angry.

"Well, then, it's just as well we are not going to continue seeing each other."

Then Max's "I'm sure that's true" sent a shiver right through her.

Penny was beginning to feel more and more out of her depth. If Max was trying to explain, he wasn't making a very good job of it.

Penny, in an exasperated tone of voice, said, "Well, if you're not willing to share anything with me then this is all for the best. Anyway, you'll soon be with someone else."

And it nearly broke her heart to think that he might be.

His "If I am, I'll make sure it'll be nothing like this" was barely audible.

And then with Penny's hurt "Max, that's not very nice!" came his almost tormented "Oh, Penny, Penny, how long do you think we can go and not see each other? Because I'd say not very long!" And now his dark searing eyes looked intently at Penny as he asked, "How long, Penny?"

He only just heard her reluctant whisper: "Not long." Then, with great self-discipline, Penny somehow resisted the temptation to say, "Max, try to make me understand – just try." But of course she said no such thing.

They drove home in an uncomfortable silence, and, once out of the car, Penny watched as without a backward glance Max crunched a few gears and drove away. But Penny did derive a certain amount of pleasure from the fact that she was pretty sure the situation Max had just found himself in was not one he was at all familiar with.

Then for one moment Penny panicked and thought, 'What have I just done?'

Now, almost reluctantly, she had to accept that when she was close to Max every sinew in her body responded to him. It was so powerful she knew he must feel it too. And yet, in spite of Max's experience, Penny could sense he didn't like it. It cast doubt on his otherwise rigid control.

Again Penny thought, 'So where, if anywhere, do we go from here?'

The next morning, listening to Simon give his daily update on how his efforts to get back with Faith were going, Penny thought, 'Well, at least they can talk to each other.' With Penny it was natural to talk openly about how she felt. She was aware that it was not always a good idea, but she reckoned that it had a better success rate than placidly accepting in silence whatever came her way. With Max that would be impossible. He would talk about wanting and needing, but he never talked about loving. And yet with Daphne and Charles he'd had the perfect example of loving, and Penny wondered what went wrong. Even if her effort had only been half-hearted, she had at least *tried* to distance herself from him. She understood that, other than with Ben, she had no experience at all, and she certainly had no experience of someone like Max; and she was beginning to see that Max had no experience of someone like her, because in spite of all that had happened, or maybe because of it, she was very much her own person, and these days she was more than a match for Max.

Alan had been at Farrington's since he was a boy, and now he was somewhere in his late forties. He still lived with his parents and although it was not for the want of trying, Alan had never had a girlfriend. Nick once said that Alan's job description should have read, 'general factotum'. The reason for this was that he was the man everyone wanted when a tap in the loo wasn't working, when a desk drawer had become stuck or even when a quick visit to the shops was needed. At any given time Alan could be anywhere, so all this depended very much on whether or not you were lucky enough to find him. He was a tall and heavily built man with a permanently red face, and he always looked harassed, which was no doubt brought on by the conscientious way in which he always applied himself to whatever job he was asked to do. This would become the most important job at Farrington's, which either amused or irritated some people, but no one was ever heard to say an unkind word about Alan. His obsessive attention to every small detail did tend to wear him out; but this was the only way that Alan could cope, so he was pretty much left to get on with things.

One morning, Nick came back from his daily visit to the service department and said that Alan had accidentally reversed a company car into the back of a customer's vehicle. The result was that the customer's car had a severely damaged boot and Alan was positively distraught. Sam said the way in which Max had dealt with the situation had almost brought tears to his eyes, and he said it wasn't the first time that he'd seen his father in Max. But whatever Max had said to Alan, he had soon calmed down.

That afternoon, after Sam had regaled everyone with his very own version of the incident, he said, "If Max is your friend, he's your friend for life – and I should know. It's a pity he has no family."

Thereupon Molly philosophically said, "There's still time."

And Sam with a casual "Maybe" went to sit in Nigel's office.

A couple of days after Penny's half-hearted attempt to call a halt to her Saturday evenings with Max, Julie asked if she would like to go on one of her singles weekends. She said they would arrive on the Saturday, and at night there was to be a dinner and dance. They would leave after lunch on the Sunday. Last year Penny had gone to a singles night with Julie and, although it had definitely not been for her, everyone had made her feel welcome. So as there had been little communication on Max's part, Penny decided she had nothing to lose and would go. Julie said the places they usually stayed were pristine five-star hotels.

Arriving at the exclusive-looking country hotel, which Penny would later find was anything but exclusive, they were met at the reception desk by Rupert and Roxene (surely not their real names). Rupert wore his long blonde hair in a ponytail, while Roxene's blonde hair was cut so short she appeared quite masculine, but they were pleasant and helpful.

The bottom half of the impressive building was covered in ivy, and the above white stonework shone like mountains of snow. It was exactly the sort of hotel that might feature on the front cover of some upmarket magazine. Inside, its soft heavy floral curtains, matching cushions and colourful carpets were all reminiscent of the 1930s. Everyone had separate bedrooms, and Julie's was next door to Penny's.

In the afternoon they went for tea in the pretty little tea room in the village. Dinner was served at seven o'clock, and the seating arrangement in the restaurant was two males and two females at each rather small table. If they were designed to create an air of easy intimacy, it worked. All the tables had name cards, and, after searching for theirs, Penny and Julie found they were sitting with Leon and Frank, who, after introducing themselves, asked if this was the first time they had been on one of these weekends. Since Julie had, this became the topic of conversation.

Leon was quite tall, slim and very softly spoken. He said his wife had died a few years ago and he was living on his own, and he said he was finding it difficult to meet someone. After listening to him for a while Penny began to think that perhaps people found his eagerness a bit off-putting.

Frank, on the other hand, had never married. Although he said he would have liked to, it had never happened. He was a large jovial man, obviously too heavy for his height. He was relaxed and easy company. He said he usually came along with Leon more for the change than anything else.

They were two friends with very different characters, but both lived on their own in similar circumstances.

During the course of the evening Frank didn't appear to make any effort to get to know anyone. He just seemed content to generally socialize.

When Penny began to notice that Leon had begun to quietly monopolize her, she felt uncomfortable, but it was when he started to speculate who would be sleeping with whom that Penny made sure he knew that she wasn't interested.

He took it well and said, "That's me sorted for the night." Then he remarked, "This set-up isn't for you, is it, Penny?"

And she agreed. She could see that for all the fun and glamour there was something rather sad and depressing about it all.

After lunch, Penny and Julie went to thank Rupert and Roxene, who all weekend had gone out of their way to be helpful. Later, after a lot of enthusiastic goodbyes, they were on their way home.

That night Penny couldn't help thinking about Max and how gentle and understanding he could be when they were alone together.

Occasionally he would tease her and say, "How do you see going to bed with someone, Penny?" And then, before she could answer, he would add, "Because I'd say a few times we've nearly being there."

And with Penny's "Oh, Max, we haven't" he'd just smile and look amused.

One morning Nigel told Penny that a week on Friday Max was going on a one-day course, and alongside this there was going to be an accountancy course. Since it was only about an hour's drive away, he suggested they cancel the postponed course and all go together, and he would drive. Nigel liked the idea and so did Penny.

Over the last weeks Max had been just the same as usual. Not seeing Penny on Saturdays hadn't appeared to bother him. In fact, Sam, who seemed to be very familiar with Max's whereabouts, said for the last three weekends Max had been in London. He hinted that Max might have a new girlfriend.

Penny consoled herself with the fact that it had always been going to happen, and she had never known what her relationship with Max really was (certainly not girlfriend). His habit of simply walking away until the next time had been difficult to understand. She was ashamed to admit that when the next time came, despite her good intentions, everything was forgotten. Sometimes when she saw Max she thought how odd it was that she could know someone so well and yet not really know him at all. But now it seemed none of it had mattered.

For some years Julie had belonged to a local walking club, and when she asked Penny if she would like to come with her one Sunday Penny said she would. Apart from the club's Tuesday outings, once a month on a Sunday the club members organized a longer, more structured walk. This Sunday it was the turn of Roger to lead the walk, and since Penny had heard a lot about Roger she was looking forward to meeting him.

When she did, he was nothing like the larger-than-life imposing man that she had imagined. The reason for this was his dramatic loss of weight, which Julie said had been on the advice of his doctor. Roger had been far too drastic in the measures he had taken, with the result that his dark-grey jacket and trousers now hung limply in resignation from his shoulders, which looked like redundant coat hangers. But there was still an air of quiet distinction about Roger. Adding to all this was his light-brown soft-leather satchel, which wrapped itself knowingly around his body and then rested delicately on his right hip. It was a silent reminder of the life that he'd once lived.

The thing that most interested Penny was the large black whistle that he wore just below his deep angular chin.

When Penny commented on this to Julie, she said, "Wait until you hear him blow the darn thing!" She said Roger frequently used it before calling out for the umpteenth time, "Not to worry, but I think we may have taken a wrong turning."

On the whole people didn't seem to mind Roger's wrong turnings.

Today the weather was dry, but with a blustery cold wind which Julie said went right through her. Everyone was hoping the walk would go without incident, and Penny overheard one or two people saying that the trouble with Roger was he would insist on leading by instinct, saying it's better than trusting those newfangled gadgets. This could have been one of the reasons that everyone thought Roger was a bit of an enigma, and the fact that he never talked about himself (apart from mentioning that he lived on his own) could have been one of the reasons he appeared to be so interesting.

Walking to a lookout point at the top of a steep incline was not easy, but the breathtaking view across the valley made it worthwhile. At this spot Roger decided they would stop for lunch, and everyone hurriedly positioned themselves with their backs against a low stone wall. As they happily ate their sandwiches they chatted together, and the bleak cold weather didn't seem to affect most of them at all. Penny, however, realized that she was well out of her comfort zone. Instead of finding it uplifting, she was actually finding it quite the opposite. Would it have been better on a bright hot day? She couldn't even begin to think about that. She had to admit she was finding it interesting, although it was not an experience she was likely to repeat.

Penny looked at Julie with her brightly coloured clothes and thought, 'You just couldn't miss Julie.'

She found herself saying that a walking club was the last thing she would have thought Julie would belong to.

But Julie said, "Look around, Penny. There's a lot of single people."

And then Penny found herself asking Julie if she had been out with any of them. She said she had, but nothing had ever come of it. Many were already in relationships or they, for whatever reason, enjoyed being on their own. The one question that Penny would really like to have asked (but she found it too delicate to approach) was whether Julie had been out with Peter. She did think if she had, she would have been only too pleased to tell her, but Julie had said nothing. After the New Year, when they had seemed to get on so well, Penny was surprised.

After dropping Julie at home Penny realized that today she had learnt a few uncomfortable truths about herself.

Sam decided that Max's disappearance at the weekends signalled that he had a new girlfriend. Sam took great delight in telling everyone once again that at Max's time of life if he found the right one he would fall hook, line and sinker. And, painful though it might be, Penny had always known that it wouldn't take Max long before he found someone else.

Then, as an afterthought, Sam added, "I'll just say this: whoever she is, she doesn't seem to be making him very happy. He's always polite, but he's even more distant than usual and he's quite impatient, which isn't really like Max."

All this time Simon had said very little, which was not like Simon at all. With Faith no longer on the scene, Nick suspected that Simon was up to his old tricks again.

One Thursday afternoon when Penny was in Max's office he said, "I gather Nigel has put you in the picture about tomorrow." When Penny said he had, Max said, "I'll pick you up about seven thirty, then. That should give us plenty of time for a 9-a.m. start."

After his cold indifference that afternoon, when it seemed to take Max all his time to speak civilly to her, Penny thought the only saving grace about tomorrow was the fact that Nigel was going. She could at least feel relaxed with Nigel.

Just as she knew he would, Max arrived at precisely 7.30 a.m. After a brief good morning, Penny said she would sit in the back so Nigel could sit beside him, and she could scarcely hear Max's "Fine!"

Nothing more was said until Nigel got into the car with a cheery "Good morning."

Penny's mood lifted. Nigel chatted to Max, and at every opportunity he brought Penny into the conversation. It seemed he wanted Max to know that he had worked alongside Penny for many years. At times outside the confines of the office his manner could seem quite flirtatious, but it was such a light relief that Penny enjoyed the banter.

The modern red-brick conference centre with its well-kept lawns and colourful flower beds had an interior that was almost clinically clean. It was the epitome of a well-run professional business.

The morning session was taken by a very impressive Tina, who certainly knew how to explain in simple terms all about the new systems that were about to be installed in their offices. At lunchtime Nigel and Penny met Max outside the larger of the two restaurants.

Over a light lunch Nigel suddenly said, "I wish I lived nearer to you, Penny, and I could have some of that hotpot you're having tonight." Yesterday she had told Nigel she was going to leave a meal to cook in a slow oven. Then laughingly he turned to Max and said, "Why don't you invite yourself in for tea, Max?"

He looked at Penny, who politely said, "If you would like to, Max," but she was relieved when he graciously declined.

"It sounds good, Penny, but I must shoot off. I've got an early start in the morning."

And Penny thought, 'That sounds right – he's away again this weekend.' A few more hours of a Max who was not particularly forthcoming was not something that Penny would have looked forward to.

Penny and Nigel's afternoon session finished at five o'clock, but Max's went on until five thirty. They waited for him in the lounge, and when Max appeared Nigel had just said something that had really made Penny laugh. Max didn't seem at all impressed.

After dropping Nigel at home, Max turned around to Penny and said, "For heaven's sake come and sit in the front; otherwise I'll feel like a bloody taxi driver."

Without a murmur Penny went to sit beside him.

Then all conversation stopped, and it took Max to say, "You're very quiet, Penny."

"No, I'm not" was Penny's quick reply.

"Well, you haven't said anything since Nigel got out of the car."

"Well, there doesn't seem very much to say!"

Max rather impatiently replied, "Well, it seems to me you had plenty to say to Nigel. In fact I'd go as far as to say you've been flirting with him all day."

"I don't flirt, Max."

In a long-suffering voice he said, "You don't? Now, why doesn't that surprise me, Penny?"

Penny ignored him. She preferred instead to say, "It's just that Nigel is so easy to talk to."

"And I'm not – is that it, Penny?"

"Max [and his heart almost missed a beat], I didn't say that, but you're . . ." And her voice trailed away.

"I'm what?"

The way she had said his name weakened his resolve to act unconcernedly.

"Well, you don't usually seem very interested and you do have a rather cold way about you, Max. You have to admit there's nothing warm and cosy about you, is there?"

Now, with eyes that were searing and knowing, he briefly turned to look at her before once more his eyes became intensely fixed on the road ahead.

But now he said, "I don't agree. I have my moments, wouldn't you say, Penny?"

And then, before she gave it any thought, she blurted out, "Only when you want something."

As soon as the words had left her lips she wished – oh, how she wished! – that she hadn't said them.

And then through gritted teeth she heard Max say, "If I wasn't driving, Penny, I'd make you sorry you ever said that."

Now the reckless side of Penny took hold, and she defiantly said, "Well, it's true!" Then, because he was driving, she suddenly felt guilty and said, "I'm sorry."

His reply was a scathing "You don't bloody well mean any such thing!" And then, just to show that he too could hit below the belt, he threw caution to the wind and cuttingly said, "Well, if I do, you're always more than willing to oblige – and don't you dare deny it, Penny!"

And of course she couldn't.

So they continued the journey in silence. Since they were driving along mostly unlit country roads, Penny thought it was just as well that Max was such a careful driver, but suddenly she heard the sound of Max's screeching brakes as he swerved on to a grass verge, narrowly missing a car that had been travelling too fast on the long and twisting road. Seemingly without a backward glance the motorist had driven right past them.

Immediately Max turned to Penny, who in her anxiety was tightly gripping the top of his leg, and in a voice that held fear and panic, yet somehow managed to sound like a caress, he urgently asked, "Penny, are you all right?" It was only after she gave a shaky yes that he gave full vent to his feelings. Then, after gently moving Penny's hand, and now seeming well in control, he gave a wry smile and said, "That was a near miss." And with a sigh of relief he went on to say, "I think I will take you up on your offer of a meal."

Penny, who was still inwardly shaking, said, "That's a good idea."

And when he gave her a reassuring smile, she felt she could forgive him almost anything.

Max locked his car door and followed Penny into the house.

He immediately said, "That's a welcoming smell, Penny."

And, without thinking, she impulsively said, "Well, you know what they say, Max – the way to a man's heart . . ." By the look on his face, he obviously didn't, and right away she regretted saying it. She hastily said, "It's just an old saying."

Max looked completely baffled.

Sometimes Penny wondered how on the one hand anyone could be so worldly-wise and yet on the other hand be so oblivious to the simple little things in life. Well, it would seem Max could.

As they sat down to eat, Penny looked at him and said, "Max, take your jacket and tie off. You look really intimidating."

He smiled. "Surely not to you, Penny?"

But he did take off his jacket and loosened his tie. He certainly seemed to enjoy his meal, and he even had a second helping of hotpot and then apple pie and custard.

The incident in the car was still very much on Penny's mind. She said it upset her to think of all the unkind things they had said to each other.

Max looked slightly amused and then gruffly said, "What are we going to do, Penny?"

And she quietly asked, "What about?"

The Max she knew surfaced, and he nonchalantly said, "Never mind!"

While Penny was making the coffee, Max came to stand beside her.

"What have you been doing these last few weeks, Penny?"

She answered truthfully, "Well, not a lot, although I have been more involved with church things."

And Max rather absently said, "Ah yes – the church."

"Now, what have you been doing, Max? Are you with someone?"

His careful reply – "No, I'm with you" – made Penny rather irritably say, "Me? You're not with me, Max. That's the problem.

I'm not part of your life. If I ask you what you are doing this weekend, you wouldn't like it. But if I was with you, I'd know. In fact you just slot me in when it suits you."

For reasons only known to himself, Max completely missed the irony of it all. He just gave an exasperated "Penny, for heaven's sake!"

However, since she felt much better for her little outburst, she pleasantly said, "Shall we have our coffee in the other room?"

And Max agreed.

Later, when he got up to leave, Penny got up too, and suddenly Max whispered, "I've missed you, Penny. Have you missed me?"

And she nodded that she had.

At first his kisses were gentle and restrained, and then as they became more demanding there was a subtle difference. Now there was an urgency that had never been there before.

More than once Penny heard Max's almost desperate "Penny, don't ever leave me." And for just one moment she could almost have believed that he really did love her.

All week Max had been his usual polite and distant self. Although Penny understood it was important to keep home and work apart, it would somehow have been reassuring if there had been just a little sign or gesture, but there had been nothing. And it didn't help that Max could so easily compartmentalize his life – it only added to the problem.

On the following Wednesday afternoon, Nigel, Molly and Penny were in a meeting with Max, and Penny thought that at times Max's attitude towards Nigel was quite belligerent. Seeing how confidently Max operated, she couldn't really believe he would ever need anyone. Then always at the back of her mind were Max's words: "For now, Penny, we enjoy each other's company." And 'For now' always hung like an angry albatross around Penny's neck. She knew she could no longer accept things as they were. She had to find the courage to finally walk away, and she also knew that the reason she was so reluctant to take that final step was the fact that Max could so easily blow hot and cold. Why, only this week, since last Friday night, Max had practically ignored her. This only confirmed to Penny that for her any other way would be disastrous.

About nine o'clock on Friday night the phone rang and Penny, thinking it was either James or Lara (nine o'clock was usually about the time one or the other would ring), she quickly picked up the receiver, only to hear, "Penny, it's Max." She was even more surprised when he asked, "If you're not doing anything tomorrow night, would you like to go out for a meal?"

She knew, no matter how difficult it was, she had to find the determination from somewhere to refuse, so she sweetly said, "Thank you, but perhaps not, Max."

And he rather abruptly replied, "Are you out?"

Penny saw no point in not being truthful.

"No, it's not that, Max. I'm going to be honest: we both want different things."

Max said, "Like what? I've said I need you – what more can you want?"

She wondered how he didn't know.

"Well, I suppose this sounds very silly, but I want to be with someone who loves me, whereas you enjoy your bachelor life and you're answerable to no one. Compromise just isn't in your nature."

"You seem to know a lot about love, Penny."

She felt he was being gently patronizing.

"I don't, Max. It's just that you seem to know very little. For all you know, you could have been in love and not even known it."

But his dry laconic "I doubt it" was very probably true.

"So there we are, Max."

Now he sounded annoyed: "This time last week you wouldn't have been saying things like this. You even admitted you wanted to sleep with me, Penny."

That was true, but now she could only say, "I'm going, Max." And then, choking back the tears, she found herself saying, "Oh, Max, why couldn't you have loved me?"

Then before he could answer, Penny put down the phone. And if she had expected him to ring again, he didn't.

She thought, 'Well, there's your answer, Penny.'

Penny hadn't heard from Max. She was out all the following day with Judi, and when she got home she checked her phone, but Max's number hadn't come up. After a shower, she put on her dressing gown and sat down to watch television, but she found there were so many things to think about she just couldn't concentrate.

About ten o'clock the phone rang. It was Max, but it was a Max that Penny was not at all familiar with. He was speaking in a slow, deliberate voice, and it seemed each word, although not exactly slurred, demanded all his attention.

So when he said, "Penny, this is Max," Penny said, "Max, you're drunk!"

And then, slowly and deliberately – only this time he sounded quite hurt – he said, "I'm not drunk, Penny." Then he paused before vaguely saying, "I think I got drunk last night, and I'm going to get very drunk later."

Penny replied, "Max, whatever is the matter?"

And now he sounded very determined: "You're what's the matter, Penny."

"Max, tell me tomorrow, when you're sober."

"Penny, I am sober."

But for Max, who always appeared to be in control, everything he was saying seemed out of character. When Penny said, "Max, you're not going to remember any of this," he firmly replied, "Oh, but I am, Penny. It's taken a few stiff whiskies to tell you how much I love you, so I'm not likely to forget. It's driving me mad." Then he tentatively asked, "You do love me, don't you?"

And Penny quietly said, "Of course I do."

Now Max couldn't stop: "Last night when you asked me why I couldn't love you and then you put the phone down, I thought if I lost you nothing would ever be the same again. You will marry me soon – you will Penny?"

"I'll marry you soon, but now go and get some black coffee."

But Max ignored this: "I didn't want to fall in love with you, but from the moment I saw you that's what I did." Now, with a sudden urge to explain all his actions, he said, "I just want to see you. It's probably just as well I can't drive, because I wouldn't want you to see me like this."

Penny replied, "Don't be silly – I'll come to you."

At this the assertive Max she knew so well said, "You're not to drive alone at this time of night!"

"I can get a taxi; and it is the holiday weekend, so I could stay."

For a split second there was silence, then his astonished "Would you?" provoked Penny's dry reply: "Well, it does seem to have taken forever to get here. Now go and sort yourself out."

But the old Max had evidently not been very far away, as he said, "I don't like being told what to do."

A more confident Penny replied, "Fine – I'll not bother coming."

To this Max slowly said, "You only tell me what to do because you love me – that's right, isn't it, Penny?"

And she humoured him by saying, "Of course it is, Max."

Although Penny desperately wanted to ask why he hadn't told her all these things before, she didn't. She realised that now, with all the time in the world to explain their many misunderstandings, that would come later.

When she arrived at Max's, he immediately came out to the car wearing black corduroy trousers and a shirt so white that it positively glowed in the night sky. He didn't look at all as though he'd been drinking. He looked the same immaculate and enigmatic Max she was so used to seeing. Max paid the taxi driver and then, taking Penny's bag and tightly holding her hand, he helped her out of the car.

Once inside the house, they looked at each other in total disbelief, and Max said, "You came!"

In the past Penny had noticed that, on the rare occasions when Max became emotional, his voice, just as it was now, had an almost smoky velvet and totally irresistible tone to it. As she walked into his outstretched arms, she felt him visibly tremble and, like a man starved of oxygen, the floodgates opened. Luckily for Penny, her ability to understand this kind and gentle but deeply complex man would prove to be the bedrock of their happy marriage.

EPILOGUE

And that was where I intended to end Penny's story, except I can't resist telling you that two years later, much to their delight and Max's boyish pride, they were the proud parents of Edward and the newly arrived Bella.